P9-CMF-572

# Stories in many Moods

First Edition



Printed by
Hugh C. MacLean Publications Limited
345-349 West Adelaide St., Toronto, Canada

# Stories in many Moods

A collection of notable
short stories by Canadian
writers first published in

The
Canadian Magazine

Hugh C. MacLean Publications Limited
345-347 Adelaide Street West, Toronto, Canada

All the stories in this book were first published in The Canadian Magazine.

# CONTENTS

# Foreword

In this modest volume are gathered together a few of the stories that have appeared in The Canadian Magazine during the past few years.

They represent stories which we think are a little out of the average run; that have a quality and feeling that justify a somewhat longer life than publication in a monthly magazine can give them.

They do not represent, by any means, the total of the stories in which we have taken particular pride. They do not even necessarily represent the best, for there are considerations that make it impossible to include all the stories that we might have wished.

But we feel that in the stories that appear here, there is a certain spirit and flavour that will appeal to a great many readers. We also know that they will not suit all tastes, for they do not lean toward stirring adventure or exaggerated plot. But those who like the stories of cadences and moods will, we feel, find in them something of the magic of story-telling.

Se we send this little volume on its way in the confident hope that it will be a means of building many new friendships.

J. L. Rutledge, editor,
Canadian Magazine.

# The Novice

## by Morley Callaghan

THE novices at recreation hour used to walk by the high brick wall dividing Dr. Stanton's property from the convent garden and whisper sincerely that soon the Mother Superior's prayers would be answered and the doctor sell his house to her. The old brick house was between the convent and the edge of the park. For five years the Mother Superior had been trying to buy it from the bigoted old man, to use it as a residence.

Once the Mistress of the novices had asked them all to pray that the doctor, who had declared definitely that his old home would never become part of such an institution, might be persuaded to change his mind. The Mistress pointed out that God was often more willing to grant favors when the prayers came from fresh eager young souls. Sister Mary Rose, who had been a novice for four weeks, and who was determined to endure all the first hardships till she one day became a nun, listened eagerly to the Mistress telling how she might help the convent. Sister Mary Rose was a well built slender girl with a round, smooth face, who looked charming in the habit with the little black cape of the novices. She was having none of the pains and the troubles of some of the novices; the plain food was almost tasteless at first but she ate hungrily; she got to like immensely the well buttered slice of bread they had at collation hour in the morning; her body ached at first from the hard bed but, to herself, she insisted that she did not feel the pains, enduring this small discomfort much more readily than Sister Perpetua, who secretly stretched her pillow out lengthwise every night so her shoulder blades and her hips would be well protected. Already two or three of the novices who had sharp pains in the back or who had lost all appetite were taking it as a sign that they really did not have a vocation and were wondering how much longer they would stay at the convent. Because she had such very good health Sister Mary Rose had the energy to hope she might be an instrument that would bring a great blessing to the convent.

So in her nightly prayers she made it almost a secret between herself and God that she was the one among the novices who was most anxious that Doctor Stanton might sell his fine house to the convent. She prayed for almost an hour, kneeling on the floor in her long nightgown, her bare heels just touching, her eyes turned toward the long narrow window looking out over the brick wall into Doctor Stanton's garden while the moonlight slanted down over her shoulders. At this time she was convinced that her prayers would be heeded more readily if she followed the precepts of St. Theresa and tried to live the life the Little Flower must have lived when she had been a novice. But she didn't ask that a shower of roses fall from heaven; she asked only that Doctor Stanton might sell his house to the convent.

For many days she prayed and fasted and was as much as possible like a little child and nearly always in a state of grace. When one of her relatives sent her a box of candies she at once gave it to the Mistress of the novices and would not even take one for herself. But she got a little thinner. She was pale and her eyes too big for her face which was hardly round now. And then at midnight, when she was sitting in her stall in the choir she fell forward on the floor, fainting.

The Mistress, an elderly, severely kind, practical woman with a finely wrinkled face said, as she rubbed her wrists, "Sister Mary Rose, you haven't been eating."

"I'm sorry," she said, still feeling dizzy, "I've been fasting to receive a favor." She sat back awkwardly in her straight backed stall.

The Mistress praised her admirable sincerity but explained it was not good for a novice to be too severe with herself. Sister Mary Rose, still weak and trembling, almost told her why she was fasting, then, shaking her head twice, determined to keep it a secret between herself and God.

As soon as she was alone she wondered if she might possibly be more effective following some other precept. After all she was concerning herself with a very material affair, a transaction in property, and she wondered if the Spanish St. Teresa, a more worldly and practical woman, who, too, had been a nun, wouldn't be more likely to assist her than little Theresa of Lisieux. So she began to think of talking, herself, to Doctor Stanton and had a kind of a vision of herself easily persuading the old man to be sensible about a business matter, and then modestly and shyly explaining to the joyful Mother Superior that she had only been an instrument because she so dearly loved the convent. But she heard that the doctor was sick, and anyway he was supposed to be a harsh, domineering man.

At the recreation hour one day she was walking by the high brick wall, past the statute of the Virgin. Some of the novices were playing catch with a tennis ball. Sister Leonarda was tossing the ball to Sister Dolores, who turned and tossed it to Sister Mary Rose. It was in the forenoon before the sun began to shine too strongly and the three novices kept on tossing the ball to each other, laughing gleefully whenever one of them missed it, finding extraordinary delight whenever one had to assume a quaint or awkward posture. The Mistress encouraged them to do that; laugh readily and joyfully for they had their long periods of silence which often left some of them moody and depressed. They were tossing the ball wildly and Sister Leonarda, the plump Italian girl, tossed it far over Sister Mary Rose's head, over the brick wall into Doctor's Stanton's garden.

The three young novices remained absolutely silent, looking at each other. And then the ball came in an arc back over the wall again. Sister Mary Rose knew that the gardener, a man with a long brown moustache, who limped, and whom she had often seen from the window, bending down over Dr. Stanton's flower beds, had returned it. At that moment she got the idea she afterwards attributed to the goodness of her Spanish St. Teresa. She walked off by herself and would not catch the ball when it was thrown to her.

Alone in the bedroom she looked out the window at the doctor's garden and saw the gardener bending over a flower bed, holding a rake upright in one hand, the other patting the earth at the base of a flower stem. The sun was shining brilliantly through the narrow window. The gardener was close to the iron fence between the street and the garden. Sister Mary Rose detached slowly from her neck a sacred medal and holding it in both hands closed her eyes, telling herself that if she carried out her plan she would be both deceitful and disobedient, but her excitement and determination only got stronger. So she assured herself earnestly, while holding the medal tightly, that her notion might be the cause of so much goodness the extent of her disobedience would be trifling compared with it. Then she said a long prayer, asking for St. Teresa's help, and urging her to be an advocate for her, in case her trifling disobedience should be misunderstood.

She asked permission to visit an aunt who lived in the city. Since she rarely asked for any kind of a favor she readily received permission. She was told that Sister Leonarda would go with her for neither a novice nor a nun ever went any place alone outside the convent.

The afternoon she was to go out she first of all

looked nervously from the window into Dr. Stanton's garden and sighed thankfully when she saw the gardener picking weeds by the fence. It was entirely necessary, if she was to be successful at all, that the gardener should be somewhere close to the street fence.

Trembling and pale, but filled with an exhilarating excitement Sister Mary Rose walked out sedately with Sister Leonarda, who was prattling gaily, glad of the opportunity to be walking in the city streets. They had come out the main entrance down the steps and were past the convent, almost to the iron fence, walking demurely, their hands folded under their little black capes, their eyes turned down to the sidewalk.

The gardener did not even glance up at them as they passed. He was bending down, his back to the fence. He had on blue overalls and suspenders over a grey shirt. They were ten feet past him when Sister Mary Rose said suddenly to Sister Leonarda, 'Please, just a second, I want to ask the gardener if he found a tennis ball I lost the other day."

"Oh, you shouldn't do that."

"Please, just a minute."

'But somebody will see you from the window."

Sister Mary Rose turned, before the startled Italian girl could detain her, left her abruptly and walked over to the fence. The gardener, hearing her, straightened up, surprised, and said, "Good afternoon, Sister."

"Good afternoon," she said timidly, hardly above a whisper, "How is the doctor?"

"Poorly, Sister, very poorly."

"Would you do something for me," she said shyly, smiling nervously. "I mean . . . Are you a Catholic?"

"No, Miss. I'm sorry though." She looked sweetly pretty with her round smooth face and her blue eyes and little black cape.

"But just the same you're a Christian, I'm sure of that," she said.

"Oh, I guess I can say that all right," he said, smiling apologetically.

"Will you take this?" she said cautiously, handing him her sacred medal, her back hiding it from Sister Leonarda.

"What'll I do with it, Sister?"

"Please bury it in the garden there. Please promise me." Her cheeks began to flush a little.

"It'll be a pleasure to do it for you if it'll amuse you," he said, smiling.

"Oh, thank you very much," she said, smiling and flustered, turning away quickly. "I'll say a prayer for you."

Sister Leonarda, who had become impatient and a little offended, said, "What on earth were you talking about?"

"He was saying he'd look especially for the ball, that's all. To be polite I asked him about the doctor."

"The doctor isn't a good man, and anyway, you know I'll have to tell Mistress."

"Please, please promise me you won't tell Mistress."

"But I ought to. That's what I'm here for."

"Please promise, little sister."

"All right," the good natured Italian girl said reluctantly. "I'll promise."

They went on talking seriously as they walked along the sidewalk, their heads held at the same angle, their hands hidden, their long black skirts swinging easily.

A week and a half later, Doctor Stanton died. He was an old man and it was inevitable that he die within a year or two. The executors of his estate wished to dispose of his property quickly and the convent made much the most attractive offer. So they were assured of getting the property.

Sister Mary Rose was ecstatically happy when she heard the convent would get the fine old house, and she was not bothered by the doctor's death. At first she prayed fervently, thanking St. Teresa for interceding for her and obtaining her favor. She could hardly resist telling the other novices about her special prayers and how she had persuaded the gardener to bury the sacred medal in the doctor's yard. She had the ecstasy from feeling that she had been an instrument, but dared not tell the Mistress about it because she had been both sly and disobedient.

It occurred to her at collation hour, when eating a thickly buttered slice of bread, that she might, in a way, have been responsible for the doctor's death by wishing for it. Though she hadn't actually wished for it, it amounted to the same thing. When she first had this thought she said to herself as she was sure her strong St. Teresa would have said, that the good of the whole convent was more important than the life of one man. But suddenly she felt weak and left the other novices, and went up to the bedroom, depressed and disturbed, wondered about her guilt or innocence.

All night she lay awake, tossing on her hard bed, rubbing her shoulders and elbows on the board till they were scraped and sore. She was wondering whether this feeling of depression and sorrow wasn't an intimation that she really had no vocation, and ought to leave the convent as two of the novices were doing at the end of the week. It was plainly her duty in this first period of her novitiate to be watchful of every circumstance which would indicate that she really did not have a vocation. First she thought miserably she ought to leave the convent at the end of the week because she was a deceitful worldly woman interested only in material affairs. And then she thought uneasily, just before she went to sleep, that perhaps, if she waited a week she might become reconciled to her own conscience, and then no one need ever know.

# To Bid You Welcome

by D. K. Findlay

THE fluid darkness of the early summer night had fallen on Willoughby Street. The syringas fringing the shadowy houses were as still as the pointing Darwin tulips. Few lights were lit; the two rows of friendly homes, usually astir with exchange of neighbours were silent and self-contained. On the Graeme verandah, Mrs. Graeme rocked herself gently, and on the steps, his back against a pillar, sat her son.

Faint scents of lilac wafted by, sweetening the underlying odour of cement pavements and watered grass. It was a street of speckless lawns but on the grounds across from them were nebulous whorls and blurs of vagueness. Mrs. Graeme guessed their cause. Confetti. There was nothing one could do about confetti. It could not be all swept up. It would remain until the leaves covered it, and then the snow. And in the springtime it would still be there among the grass roots. Always reminding . . .

The windows of the house opposite were darkened and yet there had been a wedding there that day. Guests had come from far and near; the whole street had been gay. Was this the end of Eleanor Acres' romance?

Mrs. Graeme stirred and her thoughts moved effortlessly in the quiet, remembering. A pretty child. She could see her again, playing under the maples with Jack, her own boy, a little girl with thin, agile legs, always brown, always scratched. They had been a handful those two, always getting into pickles. Once they had had a pirate's den in the Marshall's cellar and nearly frightened poor old Mr. Marshall out of his wits with their red lantern. But Eleanor was Margaret Acres' child right enough, with the same black-lashed gray eyes and the same expectant way of holding her head; believing wholly in her make-up games and paying for it in the way imaginative children do. Her games were twice as joyous, her disappointments were heart-breaks.

Her swift development had sometimes disturbed her mother. She was so eager. She lived so intensely that she grudged the night that took the light away—as if there were not days enough. But life was to be so good to Eleanor. She had planned great things for her so she was sent away early to school. Mrs. Graeme remembered the day she went, a little mite in her blue uniform who wouldn't cry because her mother must see her smiling. And for a long time afterwards, Mrs. Acres would bribe Jack with honeyed tea-biscuits to sit with her.

Ah well, that was ten years ago. The sting of that parting had faded in the glee of the first Christmas home-coming, when Eleanor, her legs an inch longer and all dissolving angles, ran in and out of the two houses in the wildest spirits. She brought over her treasures, her class pin, the middy tie she was allowed to wear as an archon, the severed coin that stood for friendship everlasting and her memory book. A memory book at thirteen! There had been many holidays since then and each time she had come home a little taller, a little prettier. And then her first beau. Mrs. Graeme smiled; it had been quite a shock to Willoughby Street. The little Acres girl was growing up.

The house opposite was always lonely without Eleanor, but her mother had decided long ago that she was to go to college. She was to have her four years of life at its gayest, gather her friendships of springing youth before she came home for good. And college for Eleanor had been all that she had imagined; rich in young laughter, escapades, enthusiasms, work and play. Mrs. Graeme saw her again as she saw her on the opening day, her peach-coloured prettiness vivid in the Autumn sunlight, thrilled and expectant. How proud Mr. Acres would have been of her. But he had died when Eleanor was a baby. She would barely remember him.

In the summer-time the Acres home moved to the tempo of youth again. There were always visitors; pretty girls with the accents of the north, south, east and west and always boys, of course. Willoughby Street had given up trying to keep track of the boys. In the evening the porch would be lively with white dresses and white flannels and laughter and the tinkle of mandolins. And along the street the parents sat comfortably, knowing where their boy or girl was that night. Her Jack, too. She could remember the very tone of his whistle as he came up the walk. "Hello, Mother . . . Oh, over at the Acres, as usual."

She had hoped that one day he and Eleanor——. But the young folks were so casual nowadays. Eleanor would stroll in, swinging a racquet, her skin a creamy biscuit brown against her light frock. "Mother Graeme! This can't go on! That long son of yours has been two-timing me again. Won't you use your influence?"

Jack would upheave his dark head with a snort. "The nerve of that Acres kid! I've asked her once, I've asked her twice and she says come and play tennis. Well, it will be some satisfaction to lick the stuffing out of you. Come on."

There were rumours, of course, about a boy she had known at college but Willoughby Street had paid no attention. Then Hugh Lomond came one day and the engagement was announced almost immediately. Every one was astonished except Jack. Sons were funny, reflected Mrs. Graeme, they knew more than they let on. But they were an ideal couple. Hugh worshipped the ground Eleanor walked on and Eleanor—she looked as if she had turned a corner and found heaven. Near them, one could feel the glow of their happiness. Hugh was a fine boy; Willoughby Street was charmed with him. Everyone knew of the Lomond wealth but it took generations, the old people said, to make a boy like that.

The night their engagement was announced, Eleanor and Hugh had walked across the street with Jack, arm in arm. They stood smiling down at her, three good-looking, friendly youngsters, all in white.

"We've brought him home, Mother Graeme, because every time I looked at him I thought, darn it, did I do right?"

"He was unsettling everything," said Hugh, grinning.

"Tomorrow," promised Jack, "I get up early and do myself a mischief."

When they were leaving, Eleanor had patted the back of his head in a way that she had. "Good old Johnny," she said. After they had gone, his mother had laid a light hand on his shoulder.

'Sorry, son."

"It's all right, Mother . . . I knew some time ago, I was out of the running. And Hugh is a good lad."

They had been married today and the street was thronged with motors and on the lawn the silk hats gleamed and the chiffons stirred with the breeze. All the little city had taken the afternoon off to see Eleanor Acres married. I had been such a pretty wedding and the young folk had made it so light-hearted. Eleanor in her ivory gown was like white marble come to like and Hugh looked so proud—and so apprehensive whenever he thought of the plans his friends were threatening. But they had let them go free in the end, with but one long stream floating behind them, and Eleanor standing up in the roadster waving joyously, a transfigured Eleanor waving until they were out of sight. A sound escaped Mrs. Graeme. Her trembling hands crushed the evening paper with its black calamitous headlines.

Her son rose abruptly and stood with unseeing, level eyes. "That corking girl," he said low, and slipped away into the darkness.

It happened very quickly. As sudden as the shadow of a bird on the grass, a shape loomed before them. Followed a sickening criss-cross of swerves and a static instant when the two cars seemed to be motionless in each other's path. Eleanor saw with photographic clarity—the white posts that lined the curve, the sun gleam on the hood of the other car and the flying figure of a nymph on its radiator cap. It grew quickly larger—large as life—it was youth incarnate, swift, shining, hair blown back by the wind! There was a faint check and jar.

"Frightened, honey?" asked Hugh.

She gave a little gasp. "Just for a minute. But nothing could happen to us today."

At the further end of the course awaited the upright figure of a man. As they swept by, he raised his hand in eager salutation, his face alight. Eleanor waved in return, smiling back at him.

"Everybody seems happy today, Hugh. Is it because we are so happy ourselves?"

"Perhaps. It's our day, you know. It's great to be done with the fuss and the fever and have you to myself at last." His glowing eyes rested for a moment on her face radiant under its smart brown toque. "Until death us do part, you know. A very satisfactory arrangement."

"I think so. Such a long time to be faithful to me, my lover, but I want every minute of it." In the kindling iris of one another's eyes, they saw their own dearness and gladness.

"Do you know, Hugh, that man reminded me of someone. I almost think it was someone I know." She looked behind but the figure had passed from view.

"You haven't told me where we are going, Hugh?"

"I'm full of plans. Tomorrow—well, that is a secret which will keep until tomorrow—but today is for our lightest whim. We will go ten miles, or twenty, or a hundred, and stop wherever we like."

Eleanor settled back contentedly. "I feel as free as the wind."

The pellucid air swam swiftly by. The world looked as if it had been newly washed; bits of it still sparkled as if with dew. The hills had swagger new coats of velvet green and the earth distilled a thousand exhilarating scents. June is the time for lovers! They passed through copses and smelled the freshness of the wood, the fragrance of bark and the light fell dappled topaze on the road.

It was a pleasantly lonesome road. The world seemer understandingly aloof from their happiness. They met no other cars nor saw any people.

"We must have come far," said Eleanor. "I don't know the country about here. Hugh, how pretty!"

The trees were closing in. Ahead of them the white and green of birch glinted against the blue-gray and bronze of beech. The wood was deeper than it seemed and the depths were filled with an unmoving intermingling of filtered light and shadow. They were conscious of a curious illusion. The trees standing straight and tall and motionless were no longer trees. They were great, fore-shortened pillars carrying on their heads, high above, the tracery of innumerable arches. Long shafts of color lay athwart them, beryl, jasper and russett, as if they came through stained glass. They felt themselves to be tiny creatures moving up an earthen aisle to an altar of blue and gold. That altar was as big as the world and when they came to it, they saw that it was the world—the blue was the open sky and the gold was a cloud in the westering sun . . .

It lay before them, dreaming in the stillness; a low rambling building with a steep roof and many gables. Little, leaded panes looked from its gray walls and the living green grass ran to the very door-step. Peace and strength flowed from it. Very old, it seemed, a house made by hands long dead, sheltering the quiet memories of human habitation. The afternoon smell of clover hung about it and the air was murmurous as with the humming of bees.

"Hugh it's perfect! There must be an orchard at the back, with gnarly old trees. Let's look, quick!"

The flagged path led them through a round opening in a tall hedge. Beyond it lay an orchard and a rose garden.

"And in full bloom too! Don't they know it's early for them, the dears!"

"Perhaps they are in bloom for you," said Hugh, smiling. "Shall we go in?"

In the vine-hung door-way, golden in the last sunshine, the door stood ajar. On the threshold, Eleanor turned to him. "What shall we find, Hugh? I have the most curious feeling. I feel—as if—we are expected."

Hugh was staring intently. "How distinct the little shadows are on the flags. And the vivid green of the grasses pushing up between them. I seem to have seen it before."

Eleanor pushed open the door. "Oh!" she cried, delighted.

Within were gathered those enduring things that have made home for man from time immemorial. In the dimness, the level shafts of sunlight fell about them. The charm of half forgotten things stirred them, like a faint memory of childhood. The cool dimness invited them.

The freshness was like a blessing. They could be neither hungry nor thirsty, tired nor dusty there.

"Where can they be?" wondered Eleanor. "There must be someone. It feels so gay, so lived-in!"

They called but only cheerful echoes returned their voices. On the mantel-piece, they found an inscription, half-obliterated by the touch of time, and it was like a welcome. Thereafter they ranged through it, exclaiming, calling to one another, darting up unexpected ways to find in the upper rooms an old, sweet smell like lavender and windows that framed the sky and the clouds. A house ready and garnished—and waiting.

Afterwards they wandered in the orchard where a breeze stirred the leaves. They were young and in love; they dallied, laughing, beneath the boughs in a happiness that was near ecstasy. The house drew them back again. It was older and wiser than they; it knew something hidden from them, some tremendous secret.

It stood strong and friendly in the gathering dusk, a roof-tree for cheerfulness and quiet content, secure against sorrow, a meeting-place of softly-flowing days and nights of dew and stars.

Eleanor looked back through the vistas of the darkling orchard.

"I wish that we could stay for always, Hugh. It is like a little corner Time forgot."

"It is like the home I planned for you some day," said Hugh.

* * *

"I'm so happy, Hugh. It has been more perfect than I dreamed."

His lips moved against her hair.

" 'The Last House' the inscription called it. I wonder why?"

They sat at a casement window watching the day die. It was not dark. The sky was like a great blue goblet from which the light was slowly draining. White petals glimmered in the garden and the leaves gave off a resiny odour.

"Hugh, Hugh!" Her voice was deep and troubled. "Do you feel it? The House is telling us!"

There were none of the little sounds an old house makes as it settles to sleep. Only a hush deeper than silence. And as through the quietness came understanding, it wrapped them round with a shadowy tenderness.

"The golden road . . . The woods like a great church. I knew what we should find beyond it. I knew there would be an orchard. I knew every tiniest detail of the Last House before we came. And Hugh," her hand tightened in his, "we were expected!"

"Yes dear, I think I'm beginning to understand."

"I'm trying to remember . . . to remember . . . something that happened . . . long ago. Hugh, are we—are we dead?"

"I don't know, dear."

"But it has all been so real, so happy."

"Yes. They have given us our day, dear. Given it to finish as we dreamed. We looked forward to it so long. Perhaps our fate couldn't be changed but they were compassionate. They gave us our day together."

"And tomorrow?"

"Tomorrow, I suppose we go back or go on. It doesn't seem to matter much now, does it? Perhaps the road out yonder is ours to take, and follow, wherever it leads. At the end of it we may find Him and then we shall know."

Her face turned to him was like a white rose in the dusk. Her voice was quiet and low. "I am not afraid now, Hugh. He has been merciful . . . Do you remember the man who was waiting by the roadside, who waved to us? I know who he was now, Hugh. It was my father."

# Son of Yonderbound

by L. Paul

FROM the bogland hills rose meanly, lacking the upsweep of other hills that I had known. Scrub timber bristled on them, and crowded the fences of the scattered clearings. Twisted cedars grew, low-branched, on the lower levels. And, skirting bog and hill, cutting across the half cleared farms, went the road that was to end at our place of meeting.

For I walked alone. Pneumonia, that enemy of the strong, had grappled with my father, tall Yonderbound. One lay he walked by my side; then had come sudden sad magic, and my father, a changed man, lay between white sheets, surrounded by those disciplined hospital decencies. In his ordeal, at first, I had found no place; later, the crisis past, and convalescence stretching ahead for weary weeks, I learned that doctors and nurses must live. And so, I had gone where money might be found. The pulpwood contractor had seemed sorry when I drove my axe into the butt of a new-felled log and asked for my time; but word had come at last. My father wrote that he was a well man; he would meet me at Alderbrook. Once again there would be places to go, things to see; and so, this twisting road I walked alone led to other roads we would walk together. This mean country was the last of my loneliness put into hill and bog, and scrub brush.

It was late, and cold for July. I quickened my pace. The sun was dropping behind the hills. The bottom lands were pools of shadow, the cedars blacker than before. Only the road lay white and dusty. And across the road something now moved, beyond that bend ahead.

It was a man, who slouched or slunk, crossing swiftly. Once he turned his face towards me, but against the sky the face, in silhouette, gave no hint of detail. Even its outline seemed softened, blurred. Then his head dropped, and his long legs writhed over the bordering fence. A clump of cedars swallowed him.

Some voice within me whispered, "You have seen this man before." But, as I came up, and noted the cropped grass within the fence, the hoof-punched ground by the slowly oozing creek, the byways twisting through the trees, I laughed away this voice. Seen him before? Ay, a hundred of him, like him. Toil-bent, a chained creature, gripped in a remorseless round of little tasks, I had met him and his fellows from coast to coast, had laughed at their seriousness, their intent worship of labor. Because a cow was lost this man would quarter this pasture, this swampy brush, till he found her; nor spare a moment to hail a stranger, though to him strangers must be a novelty.

Well, here was slavery, and I walked free; here was what my father, Yonderbound. had saved me from, when he set my feet on the open road. And here was I, a man grown at last, and my own man, at that.

I passed the cedar copse and, passing, felt that I was watched. So I turned suddenly, and bushes crackled. The man was still there, withdrawn, a shadow half seen, moving away as I stared. I heard his voice,—"So Boss! So Boss!" There was little conviction in his husky tone. Perhaps he never expected to find that cow. I walked on. Thus children on frontier farms, half wild, had hidden to spy on us footloose folk. This lonely man, in a lonely country, might be as a child. Else he would have waited to hail me, to exchange news. Instead, there he had lurked, watching, secretive, perhaps afraid. I felt a half-guilty surge of pleasure. I had grown during these years. My shoulders were broad and flat; my arms were long, well muscled; and my hands, swinging as I walked, could become easily, as they had indeed become at times, capable fists. I was a man, and this other man feared me, and that, in a measure, was greatness.

I walked on. One detail only stuck with me. He had red hair, this watcher. Only red hair, in this light, could ape the damp darkness of his head. I walked on, round a bend, and now behind me I heard the dull thud, thud of a trotting horse, like a great pulse beating nearer, louder. And the rider came into view, sitting stiff and straight on a black mount, nor drawing rein till he was upon me.

I stopped as he stopped and found myself gazing up into a broad face beneath a wide-brimmed hat, into calm eyes that gave promise of humor, though his expression now was stern. He sat there in the saddle, staring back at me. I was glad I hid no secrets—this man would have guessed them.

Suddenly a dog yelped somewhere else. He rose in his stirrups, in one stirrup, rather, for now I saw that his left leg was stiff and impotent. His voice was slow, yet seemed to carry as he cried,——

"You, Lafe, come out here!"

Then in a lower tone he added, as if owing me an explanation,——

"That's Lafe's fool hound dog. Lafe fancies himself as a hunter. But it ain't open season."

"And no deer in this man's country," said I.

"No deer," the big man agreed. "Yet huntin' o' sorts for Lafe. Wonder if he's alone."

He pondered this matter soberly, as if Lafe's doings must be interpreted in accord with weightier knowledge he possessed. When three men broke cover the big man on the horse thrust one hand suddenly, in a stabbing gesture, towards his belt; then as quickly withdrew it. He said, to himself,——

"Not yet, thank God."

And he edged his horse between me and these newcomers.

They carried rifles, wore torn faded overalls. The dog, a mongrel hound, strained at a rope leash. I prayed the leash would hold. I had met such brutes before. They did not like tramps.

The three men held their guns high, faces working, as if some hatred urged them to action. But the big man on the black horse said, "I wouldn't Lafe." That, and nothing more. Even to me it now seemed inconceivable that Lafe 'would'. For the two men with Lafe backed away, dropped their rifles to arm's length. Even the dog, seeming to sense control, stopped straining at his leash. Finally Lafe blustered,——

"You can't run me, Tod."

"Ain't aimin' to," the big man, Tod, grinned. Then he nodded meaningly towards me.

"This lad's comin' my way. Reckon we'll be gettin' on."

One more remark he threw back over his shoulder as we passed,——

"Handle them guns gentle. They might go off."

But he spoke to an empty road. Men and dog had vanished back into the brush.

"They will o' course. But I had to tell 'em," said Tod.

"Will what?" I asked.

"Men is mostly fools," was his answer. "You'd best be the exception, and come with me."

Come with him I did. What lay behind all this I could not guess. But I knew this man, knew, rather his type. Such men I had see in other places. Strong men, and wise, they ran the country store, or held county office. Or they sat outside a livery and whittled and said wise things that went from mouth to mouth till they became public belief. Or they lent money and took their honest interest, and held weaker men to honesty by taking it.

No meanness in such men. And a certain unsung greatness was theirs. For they dared to think as others wished they dare think. And when they prospered lesser folk, word-wise, not appreciating them, would dub them boobs or Babbits and dismiss them into the limbo of scorn. But those of us who knew them, valued them, as we will value them so long as strength and honesty and honor last. Their sin, of course, was that they were practical; and they lacked as much the gift of words as the self-conceit to trumpet their own praise.

Such a man now rode beside me. When the village opened up before us he said, simply, as if that settled it,——

"You'd best stop with me."

Nor did I question him. Somewhere I must stop, and this offer decided me, if offer it was, and not command. Also, I liked the man; and I guessed that, later, there would be talk. I might learn, even, what those three men hunted and why they must not hunt.

The village street was deserted, but, from doors half opened, curtains drawn aside, folk watched our passing. The big man on the horse, Tod, turned in where a square built structure stood, back from the road, at the end of a row of elms. He slid off his horse before a huge door of heavy wood, iron-studded, with a great knocker of shining brass. The horse stood there, reins dangling, western fashion. Tod walked stiffly to the door, rapped, and waited.

"Bum leg. Cork ain't flesh," said he, flicking his slack left trouser-leg with his hat.

Then the door swung wide. A little gray bearded man came out. At the sight of me he stiffened. But Tod spoke,——

"Put Nick in behind. Leave him saddled, Bud. Then lock up. We're in for the night, mebbe."

"Oh yes. We're in till . . ." Bud began, but with a look Tod warned him to silence.

Then he stumped in before me. The hall was wide and bare. A passage led off it to the rear. Down this passage we went to a wide room with heavy shutters on the windows, stout table, potbellied iron stove, and worn benches of deal. No pictures on the walls, the floor, scrubbed boards. Doors broke the blankness of those walls; what manner of folk had grooved those worn planks of the floor I could but wonder.

My eyes gave me the answer. Tod swung a narrow door wide. In the door a little wicket, ironmeshed, showed. Inside a plank bunk clung like a shelf to a partition. And, black against the sky, iron bars blocked a small slit of window.

"You'd best sleep here," said Tod. "We'll eat in a minute."

As the cell door slammed behind me I knew that this was gaol.

I had learned to hold my tongue. When you were in you were in and talk hurt rather than helped. Better let those who held you play their hand; then, watching, you could guess the game, knowing trump and trick.

So, when Tod brought me to the plank table I sat on my bench and wolfed bread and cold meat, and drank tea, and kept silent.

I hoped he would talk, guessed vaguely that he was not unfriendly. Doubtless I was to him a known element in the routine of his life, a species he saw often in his career of loosing and binding. In him there was no hate, as in other gaolers I had known. He was, I felt, too big for any such furious emotion.

When he did talk he surprised me. For he flung cards and a board on the table and asked,——

"Play crib?"

We cut for deal. The little graybearded Bud cleared the table for us. Now and then, as we settled to our game, Bud would tiptoe out along the passage, to peep from a barred window that flanked the front door, and gave on rising ground beyond the village. Like a frame that window was, the picture within it the after-glow of sunset, with three tall elms black against the sky, and open grassy ground beneath them.

We played our game listlessly. "Fifteen two, fifteen four, and one for his nob" and at last this wisdom from Tod.

"Never have eights or seven in the crib, kid. That's average. Folks guess as much. See? And a double run of three, and that's game."

But tiptoeing back from the window in front, said,—"All they need yonder's a neck." And I could see that below the three trees men now milled, a compact group. The afterglow was dying, the picture framed in the window was fading. I felt the little hairs along my neck as they took new form and stiffness, became each a tiny needle, stabbing me. I said, striving to keep my voice casual, steady,——

"There's been murder. And you . . ."

"Hell, yes. Ain't you guessed that much?" Tod replied.

"And you figure I did it?" I forced the laugh that echoed crazily through the high ceilinged room.

"No." Tod swept the cards together, into a heap. "That murder's done with. 'Tis the next I'm watchin'."

"Yourn," Bud amplified this. "Yourn, stranger. Them folks has the rope and the tree. All they lacks is the neck."

The cards lay disordered before me. A red diamond blotched the uppermost, an ace. My brain was working now, leaping unessential gaps. I remembered a man with shambling gait. And his hair had been red—red it had been. Nearly had he done for me, half-grown gaycat, in a heaving, bouncing box car, years before. The face of him had been bestial, the face of a killer. On it sprouted a fuzz of bristly red whisker.

And, today, I had glimpsed a man who shambled across a road to lurk in a cedar copse. And his face, against the bright sky, had been softened in outline, as the gray beard now softened curve and angle of Bud's face where he stood back to the dying glow of the front window. And there had been hair that shone dark as if wet, and that meant red hair. And there had been murder done.

Red Aleck, that man of memory had been, and a killer. Red Aleck, this other man I had seen today might be, for here had been a killing.

I sat there, staring at the ace of diamonds that was red. I drove my memory till Red Aleck lived again in it. And resemblance became certainty.

Tod nodded, eyes upon me. Bud crossed the room and threw open the door of a cell. A man lay there, head bandaged. On that bandage a red splotch showed.

"They nigh got this one," said Tod. "I happened by and brung him in. When folks gets panicky, there's no guessin' what they'll do. He's creased, that's all. Know him? He follers the grit."

It was my father. As I knelt, feeling for his pulse, I sensed that Tod had come behind me.

"Be none the worse in two or three days," said Tod.

"If he's here," Bud added darkly. "He has it on us. Bein' unconscious he'll never know. While us . . ."

And tiptoed again to that front window.

The mob had thickened, up there on the hill. One of them had shot my father. I hated them, but did not fear them. Only, I hoped, if conflict came, I might strike back. As if guessing my mood, Tod began to talk.

It was, of course, sheer panic that had driven them. A miser had been killed, a mean man. Such folk live with a lure that draws too often the killer. This man's fortune was sheer legend. Yet the legend had sprouted darkly into this. Someone passed by, and there was a dead body and a rifled cabin high up a hill. And each man thought, "This might have happened to me."

They had guns and, somewhere, was the killer. My father, coming to meet me, had met instead men who shot first and reasoned after. It was Tod, riding up, who had saved him.

"And now we sets on the lid of Hell, and she gets up steam," said Bud. He was, as I now guessed, Tod's deputy. Since Tod was calm he affected calmness. But the scaffold of authority that had raised him above his fellows was now shaky. But was never long away from that front window.

"Henry Larkin's speechifyin'," he said, suddenly.

"Beats hell, don't it," Tod replied, ruefully. "I've knowed Henry Larkin to drive back five miles 'cos he forgot a nickel's worth of candy for his kid. Now he'd burn this gaol, string you two up, an' if he shoots me he won't regret it for as much as half an hour. Ain't human nature confoundin'?" And he stared at me.

We had come back to the big room. I sat, hands gripping the edge of the table. Tod said,—

"You ain't scared, more likely mad. Why? What you know?"

My unconscious father, in his bunk, stirred. New realization came to me. I found myself suddenly standing by Tod, leaning down, pounding the table with one fist, crying,——

"He had red hair. He hid in the swamp. He'll be there yet. I can find him, I tell you. I can find him, must find him. Red Aleck, I tell you." And I would have gone on and on, seeking force of argument by repetition.

Tod said: "Even if there was this Red Aleck, what use'd he be, alive, you tell me that?"

"I've had his hands on my throat," I said, as if that must convince him "On my throat, and me half grown. You tell them, tell them out there, the mob, tell them the man that did it."

"And won't they laugh." Tod rose. He nodded to little Bud. "Best show the boys your artillery," said Tod.

Bud slid out of the front door. The mob on the hill was suddenly quiet. I heard a dog bark, far off, then Bud's voice, high-pitched, at breaking point,——

"This here's a riot gun. I aim to use it."

Voices surged back, drowning his,——

"Best stand clear, Bud."

"We ain't after you."

"We want them tramps, both o' them. You tell Tod."

A fire flared suddenly, up there below the trees.

"Tar barrels," Tod guessed. "No, sir, give 'em two hours to work up their nerve and a live murderer'll be no good." And he paused, staring at me, calculatingly.

"This leg ain't no good in a bog," said Tod. "I reckon I'll chance things."

He moved across the room, said, "Bud'll shoot straight behind walls. We got two hours, mebbe." And he opened the back door.

The shadow of the gaol lay, a black path, across the field, touching a gulley through which a stream crawled.

Tod said: "A man could make it." And, as I crossed the threshold, needing no second hint, I could hear him stumping back towards the front of the gaol.

Night closed round me as I dived for that gulley, as I crept beneath arched branches through shallow water, over a sandy bar, and into a culvert beneath the road. Back on the hill the mob had increased, stood packed about the fire and a man who talked and talked. Nearer someone moved on the road, a queer-sounding medley of footfalls betrayed him, "Toc-to-o-o-c, toc-t-o-o-o-c", and with this a regular clump, clump, clump, clump. A man led a horse. I waited no longer, for of course that mob would post its sentinels. I plunged on up the creek. A wire fence barred me, tore my clothes as I snaked through.

Nobody had heard me. Yonder, around that bend, was the cedar swamp, my goal. Here Tod had come upon me, on his black horse, Nick. Now another horse was coming through the night.

For the fence I leaped. Down into brush I plunged, as that other man had plunged hours ago.

I wasted no time. The rider had gone back. Had he gone for help? Had fear driven him? Yet he had less to fear than had I.

Lying there I strove for calmness. My brain worked swiftly, yet coolly now. If Red Aleck had come here, here he still would be. For the roads were dangerous even in the early darkness. Only when the night had nearly gone, when watchers grew heavy eyed, would be chance escape.

And I must find him, must quarter this wilderness through and through, till I came on him. The immensity of this task was dwarfed for me by the urge, the dire necessity of its accomplishment. Nor did I know what I would do when I found him. Tod's words lay somewhere in the back of my mind. They would surge up if I found Red Aleck, the killer. Tod had said,—". . . what use'd he be, alive? You tell me that."

I crept on beneath the low-growing cedars. There was a dim ghost of light in the clearings. Objects began to take form. A thin tracery of blackness became a fence, and beyond was cleared land, a farmhouse, and a road angling that by which I had come.

So the swamp was a 'V', narrow and long. Red Aleck would lie somewhere along its centre. Crawling, I reached the centre just as that first shot boomed, tearing the night quiet, drowning the faint little, honest little natural whispers of the place. Then cattle came snorting and splashing through a clearing and behind them something of another shape, running crouched low, angling from their course.

It was a man. I sprang for him, closed with him, felt the wet ooze on his clothes, found one hand slipping through his dank, bristly beard, and knew I had found the man I sought, nor guessed, then, why that single shot had sounded, how it had driven him across my path.

We went down in the muck, arms locking, bodies writhing. Yet I wasted precious breath to cry my triumph,——

"I'm a man now, Red Aleck. I'm a man growed."

And, that boast on my lips, found it was but a boast. For he was strong, strong and desperate. Before his eyes was the rope, and the scaffold was building for him. And nothing he need fear save defeat in this, our battle. He he kept gun or knife the thing would have ended then. But they would have been evidence; somewhere he had hidden them. Yet what he had, almost sufficed. We thrashed about there, in the cedar swamp. I felt his gaunt body arch, as I lay upon him for an instant. Then I was flung aside, and his hands were reaching for me, his knees were driving against my stomach. Then he was lifting me, then crashing down, with me, on me.

Then sight ended, for we stumbled and fell and floundered in black bog water that oozed into my eyes and blinded me. What I saw from now on was a picture that came from within, my father lying there helpless in Alderbrook gaol, the mob outside, and those three trees with the rope now pendant and slack, now taut, suddenly.

So now strength came to me; new force, with which I matched Red Aleck's frenzy, thudded home with every blow. And I broke free of his crushing arms, broke free to spring in again hammering him desperately. Yet he fought on, matching blow for blow. He too saw the rope, guessed the mob, and one more death on his hands was nothing to him, added not at all to his peril. My death, in fact, meant his chance for life.

So, when my foot slipped on a half buried root, when I went down again, spreadeagled, in the ooze, I guessed that I would never rise again. It was sheer instinct that brought my battered hands up over my eyes as his boot crushed down towards my face. And it was, therefore, in terms of sound that I sensed what now happened. Sound of some great creature crashing through the swamp brush; sound of cattle snorting, wallowing away in new fright; sound, at length, of a gunshot.

For it was Tod, Tod on his panting nigh-foundered black horse, who saved me, shooting as Red Aleck's hands groping, found my throat. And as Red Aleck collapsed, lay heavy, inert upon me, Tod said,——

"Guess you done your stuff, kid. Yeah, I figured that first shot'd flush him. Now he's kind o' useful in my business. You hoist him up here."

I writhed clear of dead Aleck, gripped his shoulders, hoisted him till Tod's strong clasp joined mine. Together we got him across the horse. Then Tod said,——

"Grab the left stirrup. I don't use it none. We're goin' to travel. Fire yonder's died down.

In that fashion, myself fagged, stumbling, holding the left stirrup, dead Aleck before him, Tod headed out of the swamp.

Down by the gaol a dark compact mass showed. The fire on the hill beneath the three elms was but a patch of glowing coals now.

A gunshot roared and lead whistled past.

"Bud's firin' high. Guess they ain't but started," said Tod. "We come in time."

His shot echoed Bud's; his lead sang as harmlessly over the heads of the mob. But now, where the mass had been solid black, white patches showed as men turned their faces towards us.

Down to them rode Tod. Myself, I staggered beside him and my weary head bumped suddenly against that artificial leg of his. In him there was betrayed at this moment no more emotion, no more apparent feeling than one could discern in that leg. Big and calm he rode, till the mob split before him, till he reached the broad stoop of the gaol.

Here he loosed his grip. Red Aleck slid to the earth, balanced there in a heap, dead stiff legs propping him for an instant. Then he rolled over, lay flat, blind eyes staring upwards, horribly, fixedly. Tod says, "What you been cravin', boys. Take a look. Ain't it purty!"

They crowded close to stare, then drew back. Red Aleck was no pretty sight. A man bent over him, fumbled in his pockets, held up a wad of crumpled soggy bills, a few stained, discolored silver coins. For these that miser had died. Little good they were to Aleck now. The mob, that great, powerful, self created machine, panic borne, had now no object. A man on the outskirts cried suddenly, "By Dad. I ain't milked my cows!"

Men laughed. And Tod said, "What's over is best forgot."

From the window of the gaol—he could not see us from its narrow barred opening—old Bud yelped, suddenly,——

"Stand back. I got another barrel."

But giant laughter shook the crowd at this. And old Bud, dropping his gun, swung the great front door wide.

Tod said, again,—"What's over is best forgot." But he would not forget and they would not forget. Once again he had proved his eternal rightness, demonstrated the quality of his leadership. By morning they would be coming to him again for his advice. In a week, to all intents and purposes, this wild night would be forgotten. Yet they would not, in their hearts, forget. And, knowing this, he would be big enough to hide from them all that he must remember.

He smiled, at last, this man of strength, and gave me one final surprise,——

"I always thought a heap of Yonderbound. You take after him, kid." Then as I made for the open door of the gaol some flicker of professional pride stirred in Tod, for he said, half serious,——

"Reckon you've slep in worse gaols'n mine."

# Mrs. Balcom's Hat

by Albert C. Trimble

ROAST beef! Red juices, delectable brown outside, crispy fat, rich gravy. To Old Anna Ryz, as Mine bare it past to the dining-room, its tantalizing smell was almost unbearable. But it was Friday. Old Anna crossed herself devoutly and sat down at the kitchen table to vegetables. Fridays—Mrs. Ballcom's day—stretched out like angry mileposts back along the years. She hated them, not even a bit of fish or an egg. She would have quit the godless Ballcoms years ago except that they paid her three dollars, elsewhere only two-and-a-half.

Mina returned with her own plate generously served, a whole round of meat. The third Friday in succession, and for a girl who had been raised by the Good Sisters! When a girl brought up in the very shadow of the church ignored fast days it spelled trouble; and she had been almost sullen of late; antagonistic. Old Anna frowned uneasily, but went on mixing creamed beans with her potatoes.

Mina fussed with her plate, making a ceremony of her preparations. "How's Paul?" she asked, reaching for the salt. "Still looking for work and hoping he won't find it?"

Making fun of him and caressing his name in the same breath!

"Joe got his good job in the bank because of his languages, and he speaks only six," she went on. "Isn't it seven Paul has? He should set up in business. You, his mother, should give him the money to set up."

"Should I, indeed?" But she would, and gladly, if he would stay set, though no Ryz ever could. "Since when is it the concern of Mina Fodchuk?"

The girl colored. At her discomfiture the old woman's hands folded complacently, and not till Mina began to eat did she take her first knifeful.

"Look out, Batcha!" Mina, still flushed, laughed disagreeably as if to ease the hurt, her shoulders shrugging so that the perfume she had taken to of late mingled with the thick smell of food. "Look out or you'll cut your throat."

"Whose throat is it, Mina Fodchuk?"

Batcha, indeed! Would not Mina like to be calling "Grandmother" to the mother of Paul, after his father the handsomest man who ever stepped in shoe leather? Mina was handsome, too, with a dark and bold beauty. What a pair Paul and she would make! What children they would have! . . . But she would rather see Paul dead than married with one whose mother had—— Old Anna's food made horrid strangling noises in her throat. It choked her even to think of Cassie Fodchuk, the mother of Mina—Mina, the living image of her, sitting there eating meat as coolly as if there were no such office as confession, playing the lady with her little finger and the cerise handkerchief in her wrist-watch band. Lady! when everyone knew what the Fodchuks were, part White Russian, their grandfather in jail. Mary be praised, never a Ryz had been behind the bars. Though once, when Paul had wired her for two hundred dollars in great haste—— She crossed herself again, her ears absently cocked towards Mina whom Mrs. Ballcom had summoned to the telephone. Bah! these Ballcoms . . .

The sun flamed on the tree tops, its beauty tugging vaguely at her starved old heart as she trudged home with the paper sack of scraps: broken cake, and the remains of the beef, Mr. Ballcom too fussy to eat cold meat. There were usually good scraps on Fridays. "For your hens," Mrs. Ballcom would explain, saving her face. As if she cared! Mina had spoiled it this afternoon. "I know down what old hen's gullet most of it will go," she had laughed hysterically. Mina had been volubly excited from the moment of her telephone call, whatever it had been. She had been given the rest of the day off, so had missed the parting words the mother of Paul had planned.

Parting words. Munching sunflower seeds from the supply in her sweater pocket, Old Anna chuckled. It was a good joke on Mrs. Ballcom, not having given notice that she was through. Let her get the washing ready next week, and wait. Wait and wait, then drive around in her fine car. Vegetables, indeed! Fish and eggs she would have on Friday from now on.

It was a pretty day, leaves falling in brown and gold, the osiers blazing red; and it was made prettier by her thoughts. Inside her clumsy shoes as she trudged over the pavement her feet seemed to dance. Forty-eight, but experiencing a strange recurrence of her emotions at eighteen. Paul in her arms down in the vile-smelling steerage, her labor done . . .

Now her little shack was in sight. The mile had been no distance; because, she gloated, it would not have to be traversed again. She felt like taking off her hat and shouting to the few persons in the street, "See me, here! I'm not Mrs. Ballcom's 'Old Anna' any more; I'm not anyone's 'Old Anna' any more; I'm my own." But she did not. She could lay no real claim to herself while she wore this hat, Mrs. Ballcom's hat, for Fridays. Years of cast-off hats. Hats! And she with three beautiful platoks at home.

Yet she did own herself. She was her own Old Anna. Had she not saved her thousand dollars? Thirty years of scrimping and saving; her three-roomed shack to pay for; the old mother-in-law to nurse and bury; Michel himself to bury that last time he returned; above all, Paul to educate. The trouble with Paul, she thought uneasily as she reached for the gate latch, was that she had given him too much education. Handsome as his father, was he as unstable?

She could barely wait till inside the gate to take off the hat. "You ugliness!" she apostrophized the dingy straw of a bygone floppy style, its roses faded and frayed. No wonder such as the Fodchuks said she had no pride, though little they knew of the meaning of the word. Settling the paper sack on the back step, oblivious of her scurrying hens, she marched to the alley and removed the garbage can lid.

"There!"

Into the emptied can she crushed the despised headgear. The bottom of the garbage can, always lined with paper, was now lined with Mrs. Ballcom's hat. With her hands on her hips she threw back her head and laughed loud and long. Let the neighbors, especially the bedridden Katya Sawchuk, next door, think she was crazy. Perhaps she was. Though anyone would laugh to see Mrs. Ballcom's hat flattened out grotesquely against the bottom of her garbage can. Tomorrow she would put all the other hats with it: Mrs. Pritcher's green velvet, Mrs. Sloane's brown tam—how did she call it? berry, was it? anyhow, it was better on her than framing Mrs. Sloane's smug, fat face. How she hated them all! But no more; the badge of Mrs. Ballcom's servitude abased. She drew in long breaths of the nippy air.

Now, she noticed her hens. Clustering around her as if for protection, their shrill welcome was comforting. A sparse flock of late, she thought uneasily, peering into the nests. Not an egg. Less every day, Paul's weakness fried chicken, an extravagant way to cook good fowl. But it made him happy, if it would coax him to stay and settle down! "Though," she told herself grimly as she stopped to gather a few ears of corn, the husks dry and withered from the frost, "no Ryz was much in that line."

The big room had a rumpled look. The blinds, let up to the top, all askew, gave the room a glaring rakishness. The fire was dead, empty bottles and glasses making rings of dullness on her polished range. In two glasses on the table were the dregs of wine. Wine! Celebrating? Michel had always made a feast before he went, if only a feast of music on his fiddle to set the pace for his roving blood. Her heart contracted. Was Paul going again . . .?

Casting her fear aside, she sniffed the smell of cigarettes and beer; not even good beer, probably the brew of Old Grandma Fodchuk who was running the still in her lord's absence. Joe Fodchuk had been hanging about ever since Paul returned this last time, trying to persuade him to something; evil, if a Fodchuk had a hand in it. She might have put her savings in the bank had not Joe been employed there.

No, that was not so, she admitted as she propped the front door open with a chair. She enjoyed her reputation of miser, of having untold wealth hidden away. It brought her respect, a certain homage. Even the recollection of the awe with which the children stared as she passed caused her head to lift in pride.

Her money was in as safe a place as the bank, in back of Michel's picture. She looked up at it hanging between the holy pictures. As usual it was crooked from the passing of the noon express.

Straightening it recalled the day the portraiture agent had delivered it to her, though at the time her shack, not paid for, was eating up interest at eight per cent. It had seemed that he had given into her hands not a picture, but Michel himself, a Michel who nevermore would roam.

Sweeping aside the litter of papers on the couch, she sat heavily down and began taking off her shoes, ugly shoes with turned-up toes—Mrs. Pritcher's George had big feet for a boy of eleven—her eyes smiling worshipfully. She did not see the smirking face of the crayon enlargement; she saw Michel. In the mellow afternoon the red of his hair, the laughter in his wide face, the giant stature of him, rose before her with a vividness draining her of strength. It brought back his impetuous courting, the ease with which he had over-ridden his mother's objection to selling the old place so that they three could come to America and acquire wealth. Wealth? Bah! She had known hard times in the old land, but never as hard times as in this new country of whose language they three had not known a word, where they accepted scraps because they had to, not as now because she would . . . Her dread of charity, of being on the parish again, had set her goal high.

And—she wriggled her freed toes in content—she had achieved it. A thousand dollars—the three dollars in her pocket made up the sum. Back of Michel's face were nine hundred-dollar bills, nine tens, and seven ones. She liked the idea of it there, as if after all he had provided for her, had guaranteed her future. God knew she had little enough of peace while he was alive. And now Paul. With a sigh she rose.

The big room was tidied, the fire crackling merrily, the kettle on the boil. She laid the table and put the teapot to warm. Still no Paul. Should she put her three dollars with the rest? No; he might come. She would wait till morning, then change her ten ones for a ten, her ten tens for a hundred. Perhaps she could change her ten hundreds for a thousand-dollar bill. Beautiful! Beautiful! She could see herself in the bank doing it, comfortable valenka on her feet, a platok on her head. Which one?

She shuffled into her darkened bedroom, and feeling about in the heavy oaken chest, brought them out eagerly: three, the white one yellowed, the black one greenish, the purple one faded to a murky buff. But the colors of the flowers were still brave, as brave and gay as the memory of Michel's caresses when the shawls were new. She drew a chair to the stove, her feet in the oven.

Ah! this was good! Lots of this sitting with her feet in the oven from now on, she thought fondling the still-rolled shawls. Her rheumatism would be better, her hands not in water all the time. She looked at them—shrivelled leather leaves. Her shoulder which had been giving such trouble would now be fine. Only taxes to worry about. With her garden; her hens; what she could earn plucking fowl for the lazy society women, stripping the feathers, washing them, selling them for pillows and quilts—— She might get a cow and sell milk. Ah, she would be well off, she and her Paul.

Not that she could count on him. He had said yesterday that he was "fed up with this dead burg." He had been home for four months, his longest stay yet since his first departure. Was there more than his mother and fried chicken holding him? Was it that—that Mina? Tcha! Bold and luscious, sure to attract Paul who had his father's blood. Well, she thought complacently, she herself had not looked unlike that in her youth, though who would suppose so now.

If it were not for having a place to which Paul could always come, she would return to the home of her youth. With her thousand dollars, the proceeds of the sale of her shack besides, she could live as a queen in the Old Country. She might have the priest write: see what friends were left, Sonia Masyrik and Tony Popiel, Olga Baranowicz, Magdalena Charkus, Marya Kozyk now a great grandmother. Marya had been with her the day Michel had brought her the white shawl, the day she had said yes to him. She took it up tenderly, shook it out. From its folds fell Paul's christening robe. She frowned. How had it come there?

Ah, beautiful robe! Long; to the floor from Michel's arm that day; wide embroidery of red and blue with bands of golden yellow. None of your colorless christening gowns such as Mrs. Fleming had in last week's wash, not the length of a shift, and sheer—no body at all, and "No starch, please, Anna. No; none at all." Bah! This robe, Paul's, when new would stand of itself and almost support the child. She remembered Michel's pride that day; Michel who had no use for church or priest, Michel looking like a god to be worshipped as he stood before the font, the Mother of the Holy Infant smiling upon him from Her niche. It was not She alone who smiled; even then, Cassie Fodchuk, big with Joe, had her eyes on him.

But she had vowed not to think of that. Here with this robe on her lap, she would think of Paul's children. Many, she hoped, to use Paul's infant things stored away—the silver rattle Michel had sent him when he was four. That was Michel, the days and weeks and months nothing to him; strolling in as nonchalantly after an absence of years as if he had been merely to the corner for tobacco. Sauntering in, taking her again to his heart . . .

Still in a glow yet strangely uneasy, she moved when Paul returned. He was dressed as if for a wedding. With that silly flower in his buttonhole, he might have been the bridegroom.

"Mother," abruptly, "give me five hundred dollars. I must have it; at once."

Trouble? Was that what shook his voice and paled his ruddy face? Or was it that he was slightly drunk? She paled, too, but feigned indifference.

"Tcha! Don't make play of your old mother! Where could I lay hands on such a sum?"

"Such a sum! Pooh! Joe says you have thousands hidden away. He knows. He says you come into the bank often and get big bills for small ones."

Ah, even Joe thought her rich! Good! Well, suppose she had the money, just suppose—not that she had, of course, but she might know where it could be got—what did he want it for? . . . To set up in business? Not to do with Joe, eh? No bootlegging tricks? . . . A bookstore! Where was this bookstore? . . . Not here. Out West. Then, no, she could not consider it. If it were to keep him home where he could help—She was old; not so old in years, perhaps, but in struggle. She had worked hard—look at her hands, knotted and crippled and hard; look at herself, weazened, shrunk and shrunk and shrunk. Tcha! Was he not big and strong, better able to work than she?

Paul hung his head. (His father's trick, that!) He mumbled. Perhaps it was not business. Perhaps it was a little trouble. Suppose that he had to get out, then what? How would she relish that? Say, trouble with a girl . . . Yes, if she must know—he choked on the name—Mina Fodchuk, her brother on his trail.

Old Anna's heart seemed to stop. Mina Fodchuk, whose mother had stolen Michel. Now the daughter would steal the son. She put her hand on Paul's arm as if to assure herself of reality, that she had heard aright.

"Are you—are you going to—to make marriage with her?"

"Pips might fly. Likely a Ryz would marry a Fodchuk."

Anna's heart rose. She sighed in deep relief. Too bad Cassie Fodchuk could not look up from the everlasting fire and see her daughter now.

"But even a pig would grow wings," Paul went on, his gaze narrowing in speculation, "if it were driven too hard."

Anna stood back and contemplated him glowering there, pride welling up in her at the sight. He was handsome, her boy and Michel's. Should his own mother drive him too hard? Five hundred dollars. She moved to face the picture, saw Paul eyeing her, and stammered a remark about his resemblance to his father.

He was his father over again, she said positively, and at the saying of it doubts rose afresh. If he were, was his story true? With Michel it had been lies, lies, lies; often not a grain of truth; and, at his worst, when his deceit was deepest dyed, candour in his face as in Paul's now.

"No," she said then. "Let Mina Fodchuk look out for herself, bound from her conception to come to a bad end."

Paul made to protest but muffled it. He was not afraid of Mina. What could she do? It was Joe he feared. Joe would not put up with any monkeyshines, he said; and he had something up his sleeve; a scheme to get rich quick . . . Yes, it was, if she had to know: a plan for robbing the bank. Joe needed his help. He demanded it in return for—well, for letting him alone. If his mother did not come across, he would have to give in to Joe, the only way to hold him off.

So! There was a grain of truth. She had overheard part of Joe's furtive talk the other night; his repeating, "Inside job." She could see it all: Paul, the tool; Joe turning state's evidence; Paul behind the bars. A Ryz, in jail. Oh, those Fodchuks! Well, give her time to think. It was a lot of money . . .

Paul went into his bedroom, his sullenness overflowing through the house. She could not bear it, his suffering, his agony of fear; Ryz fear which her pride could not comprehend.

It could not be as bad as he made out. Girls such as Mina—He would feel better when he ate. She could enjoy her own supper, only vegetables for lunch. She bustled about getting out some onions to slice, a dish of cranberry jelly. She drained the corn, cut bread, set the tea to steep. She wished she were a good cook. But she had never learned. In the old country, so little foodstuffs; here, scrub and wash, nothing but scrub and wash. All she knew, she felt bitterly, was scrub and wash.

It was Cassie Fodchuk who had been the cook. She had worked in a grand hotel. There, Old Anna frowned darkly, she had learned more than the cooking, too . . . It was as if it were yesterday, how she could recall making the twelfth birthday cake for Paul, candles and everything; and Michel had said, "Let's get Cassie Fodchuk to make the party; she's the girl that can cook. Let's have it a spread!" So! They had had it a spread: baked chickens, American pies, great platters of steaming galumpka. Michel had fiddled for their dancing. She could see him yet, crouched over his fiddle, playing that wild Tzigane thing of his own, his pupils beneath their long heavy lashes smouldering after Cassie, her eyes tossed to him. And the next morning, though Mina was but six weeks old, they had gone off.

They had gone off, he with his fiddle, she with her castanets; two gypsies. She would not be like Cassie Fodchuk, loose, for anything; and yet—She had gone with them in spirit: Michel marching along with his enormous stride, his face raised to the wind which threw his hair back in a red plume, his deeper red beard a beacon pointing the way. "I follow my beard," he would bellow in his rollicking laugh as he reached for his fiddle; and when he reached for it, that way, and played certain things, that way, she knew that he would take up his foot and follow it in a few days . . . Two gypsies, Cassie's face raised too, her feet dancing as wings. And then, on a roadside perhaps, she had borne him a child which had died, as she had died; and Michel had come home for the last time, his violin stilled . . .

Ah, Paul would not go. He could not, without money. All the time she prepared their meal, no dance left in her aching feet, she was aware of her power because of her wealth. Michel's wealth. She smiled at the picture as she summoned Paul who called out that he would be there in a moment; and had he forgotten to tell her that Katya Sawchuk wished her to step in immediately she was home? "Very important."

It could be nothing of great importance, she grumbled as she put on her shoes, but it would give her a chance to think before facing Paul again. The caught up the green shawl and threw it luxuriantly about her shoulders . . . Five hundred dollars. Perhaps she should give it to him. She might not live long, anyway. Better to give it when the need was upon him than to bequeath it when his need was done—if, a Ryz, his need would ever be done, Ah, Maria! half a lifetime's savings to be rid of another of the hated tribe of thieves who had robbed her before . . .

Katya was surprised to see her. Paul had made a mistake. But sit down, sit down, the day was so long here alone.

Old Anna sat down and said yes and no to the questions flowing as water. No Paul had not a job yet . . . Yes, he liked it with his mother, but a man must work . . . No, he thought of going away; soon . . . Yes, out West, he might buy a business . . . Perhaps a bookstore; he knew much about books and the like . . . No, she would not go with him yet awhile . . . Marriage in the air? Tcha!

"No?" questioned Katya smugly. "Feodor Balak's Tony saw your Paul and Mina Fodchuk walking out of Judge Thornber's office this afternoon. Civil marriage, eh?"

Old Anna managed a scornful grunt. Gossip, sure of a welcome, flew on wings to Katya!

"Can't a man make a walk out from Judge Thornber's without the world cackling 'civil marriage?' Wasn't it two years my Paul was at the law there? Isn't it yet already that Judge Thornber begs him to return, seven languages he speaks and writes, and clients of all tongues? Bah! As for that Mina Fodchuk walking from out beside him— Perhaps now she tries to have from the jail removed her grandfather. The jail does no good to such as old as Josef Donylyshyn."

"Does one wear a flower in his buttonhole to seek a job?"

"Bah!" she spat, though cold within (This Katya Shawchuk clack-clack-clacking like a hen on a china egg!) "If I told all I could tell, everyone would be as wise as I and the world too full of wisdom."

She drew her shawl closely about her and looked very knowing as she scuttled out, but she was trembling when she reached her own door. What was this closing in about her threatening the foundations of her pride? Gossip touching her who had addressed letters to herself with money in them so that her neighbors should think Paul a good son; who had mailed letters to fictitious addresses. If ever they found out that never had she known where he was; that never a step in the night but might he his; that—

The picture was crooked again; very crooked. But she could not touch it. The silence was too oppressive; it held her in its grip. Her shawl dropped to the floor.

"Paul!"

No answer. Not in his bedroom. Nor were his things. Nothing. Everything cleaned out. Nothing left to show he had ever been home, except the smell of cigarettes. That and another smell, a mocking perfume. Mina's.

Imagination, she assured herself stoutly. She had been thinking about Mina, hating her so hard — But this was not imagination, this cerise thing, a purposeful blotch on the counterpane, like Min's patronizing laugh as she had called good-bye down the basement stairs this afternoon. She swept the handkerchief fiercely to the floor and went out.

As if from her everything had been drawn, a queer weakness assailed her, leaving her as empty, withered and dry as the corn husks there in the pail. Rummaged more than rumpled the room had been when she came from her day's work. Rummaged. She saw that now. The picture, crooked—at that angle the face leered. She made to straighten it but suddenly remembered: there had been no train since she had straightened it before. With icy fingers she took it down. The money was gone. Gone . . .

Ages and ages she stood there, a mummy clasping the frame, till a rumbling startled her. Automatically she put the picture on its hook. The rumbling increased, shook her, shook the holy pictures till their bleeding hearts seemed to pulse. It was the evening train. She turned to the window in time to see the rear coach go by. On the rear platform, brightened by the last luminosity of the setting sun, were Mina and Paul, his arm about her shoulders. Old Anna stumbled back to her chair.

Old Anna. She huddled there, her brain numb with a ferment of pictures, flashes from past and future, bliss and despair, ecstasy and pain. Her Paul! Her Paul!

Darkness came on, lights across the way, a radio. In her apron pocket her hand twitched on—What! Three one dollar bills. She peered at them stupidly. Once before she had been left with only three dollars in the world. That was after she had paid for Michel's funeral and masses for his soul. But then her heart had been at ease, for in death Michel was all hers. And there had been Paul, all hers, too. In High School, but sweet; sweet, strong and sturdy, his red-gold curls brightening her homecomings at night. Now, this! His sweetness and strength for a Fodchuk. Mina's Paul. An evil Paul of Mina's ill-fashioning. O Mother of God! Mother of God!

The bills, crackling in her slowly unclenching hand, pricked her consciousness. There was something she must do at once. What? Something about a hat, was it not? A hat. A floppy black hat with faded roses. Feverishly she ran out into the moonlight to get it, in her haste tripping over the box of bottles, disturbing her fowl. The cock crowed, shrilly.

Stumbling in out of the darkness, she was blinded by the drop-light still swinging pendulumwise. Everything in the room had a strange unreality; the stove too black, the linoleum too green, the wallpaper too hideously red. The hat, also; the straw dingier than ever, the roses more dun. Suddenly it epitomized all that had hurt her in life; servility and patronage, snooping and spying, the constant pricks of scorn. But no one knew about her money; no one need ever know!

She brushed the hat carefully with her sleeve, smoothed the wide brim, puffed out the crown, furled the petals of the flowers. At an unconsciously jaunty tilt she put it on and sat down to her meal.

# From Such a Marriage

## by Beryl Gray

WITHIN the minds of all who knew them, it was utterly inconceivable that anything either good or beautiful could ever rise from such a marriage as that of Mart Matthews or Lettie Stuart. For, to all intents, there was nothing in their lives to lift either of them from deadly mediocrity, and theirs had been a marriage born of selfishness alone. Selfish on both sides, for Mart, since the death of his weary, unsmiling mother, and the subsequent scattering of his elder brothers, had lived quite by himself on the shabby little farm; and all he wanted now was someone who could cook and scrub—in short, someone to be a slave to his desires and needs. His mother had been a dreary slave; and now he knew of little other use for women. And as for Lettie—all she wanted was a home; a chance to call herself "Mrs", and an urgent wish to flaunt her married state before her associates in the dingy Harville "five and ten"—associates who talked loud voiced about their many conquests and laughed with ill concealed scorn at her own attempts to make herself as popular. For Lettie was undoubtedly a cheap little thing, raised under the doubtful care of a married sister—a sister who, in the frequent absence of her salesman husband, held no fixed standards of conventional conduct, and who treated her children with an obvious sense of resentment and distaste. Lettie, brought up on badly prepared foods, late hours, constant strife, and lax behaviour was underfed and sallow; any natural prettiness obliterated by ill health and poor cosmetics—and with only one desire in life—to "put it over them" by the possession of a man all of her own. Mart, briefly visiting an aunt in town, saw in her nothing either lovely or appealing; only an artificial, straggling young thing who by reason of her absurd giggles and upward glances, obviously had succumbed to his tall straightness—for Mart was handsome in a big, fair, surly fashion—and who could be trained to be useful in a domestic sort of way. She saw deliverance from the howls of her sister's children, a chance to show off, and both were utterly ignorant of just what such a marriage might mean. Both eager to rush headlong, unthinkingly into a bondage of which they knew almost nothing—and perhaps their only excuse their pitiable youth. For Mart was only twenty, and Lettie two years less. And so indeed, of such poor stuff, what decent outcome could be expected.

A success. It was almost inevitable that it could never be that. For there was nothing behind it other than a sense of disillusioned resentment. Mart—when he found her lacking in all domestic talents; that she was shrill in protest and unwilling. And Lettie, when she realized the dreary dullness of the farm; and that her husband was sullen, aggrieved and domineering.

Perhaps at first, unconsciously, they had tried a little. For Mart had been rather proud of the fact that he, the youngest of his family, had a home, a horse and cart, two cows, a litter of young pigs, five acres in cultivation, a battered open car, and now a wife to round it off. It gave him a rather pleasurable sense of power and responsibility. And Lettie did not know then that local girls sniffed at the mere mention of his name . . ." he's just so sulky and selfish he'd treat his wife like dirt . . .!" Just at first Mart had held her with almost fierce caresses—and satifaction caught her at the thought that as his chosen wife, the girls could never laugh at her again.

The first real storm broke quite suddenly as a climax to the smouldering resentment, and brought about through Lettie's injudicious use of rouge and powder. He must have known that she used it, but had never actually watched her until that day in May when he had come into the kitchen, and had leaned heavily against the table, eyes dark and intent, as she stood busily engaged before the mirror.

"I guess you needn't use that stuff round here!" The unexpected finality of his voice startled her. She spun around, lipstick in hand. "Why not?"

He stared at the result of her incompleted task, frowning. "Because you're my wife I guess," with a heaviness that in his desire to speak plainly was more reflective than wholly imperative. "And I don't like it."

"Well, is that so, Mart Matthews!" A flame of unaided colour touched her one white cheek. Her hands reached her hips and she drew herself erect. "I guess maybe there's lots I don't like about you, too. You can't come round here bossing me like that."

"Oh! So that's how you feel." In that moment something hard and outraged glittered in his own eyes. For a moment the savage intensity of their stare held, and then Lettie turned and deliberately raised her hand to her face again. There was a tense silence, and then Mart stroke forward and seized her wrist. "Will you wash your face or will I?" grimly. She twisted about. "You let me be, Mart, or I'll . . . !" She caught at his hair with her free hand. For the moment they were nothing more than furious, undisciplined children as they struggled—and then he flung her in a chair, staring with disapproval at her limp weakness. "Gosh, you're a pretty feeble sort of specimen!" he commented bitterly—and perhaps, because somewhere deep within he knew it was not wholly proper to treat any woman with physical violence, a half shamed colour filled his cheeks. "You make me sick!" he snapped out suddenly, and left the room. "And I hate you—you brute! I'll leave you and I won't come back!" Her voice rose to a shrill crescendo. "Think I care!" from outside, harshly, at the moment she knew he meant it, too.

Only she didn't leave. She could not have faced her sister and the girls. Could not have endured the thought that they should consider her so poor a thing that her marriage was already a failure. Cowardly enough in that respect—for there was no sense of duty or loyalty then; she nevertheless rose to her feet and finished her facial adornment, lips tight set. She would teach Mart to see that she was not to be coerced or bullied. If, through her folly, she were forced to stay in this unlovely place, she would at least do as she liked. She set the supper table almost viciously—boiled vegetable and rice—for Mart, with scornful wonder at her ignorance, had shown her what simple things he knew himself. And then she sat to wait his coming, despite herself half frightened. For she knew nothing of what he might do, once aroused, and no one near to whom she could fly for aid.

But she need not have feared violence. Mart took one glance as he sat down, and then without a word, rose to his feet, plate in hand, and walked out of the kitchen door, sitting on the back steps to eat his meal in stubborn silence. To any older person it might all have seemed very ridiculous; but the hot color burned in Lettie's face, and all at once she could not eat. For no one had ever taught her any lessons on over-artificiality, and Mart had never said a word about her appearance before. The utter distaste in his eyes amazed her with its sudden sense of shock. For a long time she sat motionless watching the rough fair head and broad back outside, and all at once she sprang to her feet. "Mart!" and she stepped swiftly outside, too. "I tell you what." She was trembling most unreasonably. "I'll wash my face if you'll wash your hair—and keep it nice. That's only fair."

"Huh!" He looked up, startled, suspicion in his eyes. "What's wrong with my hair I'd like to know. Didn't I put it under the tap this morning!"

"I guess it looks as wrong to me as my face does to you." Lettie replied with unaccustomed vigor. "It's rough and dry—and tangled too, I'll bet. Just let me see . . . !" Before he had realized she had pulled a comb from her pocket, and dug the teeth into his hair, tugging with almost furious jerks.

"Say!" He sprang to his feet, eyes ablaze. "What's the big idea!" She stepped back, and in that instant her own stare was coolly triumphant. "Will you wash your hair Mart Matthews, or will I?"

For an instant his jaw set ominously, and then quite surprisingly he flung his head and laughed. "Sure. Go ahead," abruptly. "Only give me my pudding first, that's all."

She had obviously not expected that acquiescence—and he knew it very well. But some almost unfamiliar thing deep within made her rise to the occasion, and perhaps it was an unsuspected sense of sportsmanship that made her slip into the kitchen and rub her own face vigorously before she touched Mart's hair. Only it was with subsequent increased anger and resentment that she finally set to work. It was doubtful whether Mart had ever been subjected to such a rubbing and rinsing. Lettie, once started, took an almost elemental delight in being as rough as she could, finally rubbing with a towel until her cheeks glowed and she was quite breathless. And all at once Mart once more flung up his hitherto so astonishing docile head. "Say—let's feel that muscle . . ." and his hand reached out for her thin white arm. In that moment the evening sun caught the newly awakened colour of his hair; and Lettie barely felt his hand as she stared. "Gee!" All at once, unconsciously her fingers touched the soft bright waviness. "It's pretty, Mart," and drew back, startled, as his hand gripped her arm more tightly. "You—look different, don't you Lettie? I . . . that's how I'd like you to look . . ."

They stared again—eyes wide, lips parted; and in that moment perhaps the first stray gleam of what life together might mean, touched their souls. But love could not be born of bright gold hair and pink cheeks alone—and next morning they were quarrelling fiercely over the fact that she had burned the porridge, and that Mart wanted her to learn to feed the pigs. One quarrel after another that seemed to deepen as the days went by. Once, two of the girls drove out with a boy friend; and stared with frank curiosity at the drab farm, and at Lettie's pale cheeks. "Looks like you might be kept pretty busy!" one of them laughed with a deliberate loudness. And Lettie, who had been covered with shame and confusion at being found, paintless and powderless, shabbily dressed, and sweeping the verandah, suddenly tilted her head high. "Maybe I like being busy." Desperately she laughed herself, for to the last she would not let them see how dreadful a failure her marriage was. "Maybe there's lots more that's away more intersting than in the City." It required an effort that was summoned out of her extreme necessity to make that sound convincing —hard to act as guide, show them the horse and the little pigs as if they were her dearest treasures—to make them tea and talk as if she were the happiest of housewives. It required something even more than that to go to Mart as he came in, suspicious, and heated from his outside labours, and slip her hand through his arm. "Mart, meet my friends, won't you." So surprised, that for a moment he was passive, and as they talked, almost agreeable. Even showed them round himself, and let the girls be led, shrieking round the yard, on the horse. They must have been impressed with the bronze bareness of his arms and neck, the strong, hard healthiness and the brightness of his hair—for oddly enough Mart had not forgotten that strange lesson; and one of the girls, shallow and silly as she might have been, whispered in Lettie's ear at parting. "I'd maybe put up with a lot myself to have a guy as keen as that!" Lettie's answering smile was even more stiff and unnatural. It was even worse when later, after supper, Mart rose to his feet and stared down at her, dark eyes scornful. "I like the way you show me off before your friends. You'd treat me like dirt any other time!"

For a moment her eyes opened with genuine astonishment, and then she stiffened as the force of that shot home. "Well, and how do you treat me I'd like to know." Her voice was sharp.

"Treat you!" and he laughed, almost bitterly. "Darn well I'd say, for anyone who's as little use around a place."

"Say! Anyone would think you only married me so I could work for you. I guess that's right enough, too."

It was put only in thoughtless fury, but Mart's cheeks suddenly stung with dark colour; and there was a sense of almost inexplicable guilt. But that was nonsense, and his retort was quick. "I guess as far as that goes, you only married me to suit yourself!"

"Well then, I was crazy!" But she could not deny it, any more than he could; and as their glances met, just for the moment something almost perplexed overshadowed the anger. But only for a moment; then Mart turned, and with a muttered exclamation, left the house. Lettie's face was white as she stared after him. She did not understand that queer sense of hurt, either; for they had brought it on themselves, and had no reason to expect anything better. And while Mart kicked things in the stable savagely, and wondered moodily at some oppressive weight within, Lettie stood in silence, and with an utter, new terror in her soul. For after all, to be eighteen, to have no one who could understand or counsel; to be confronted with a dreadful possibility—and a man who looked like that her only refuge . . . it was enough to strike a note of panic in an infinitely stronger heart than Lettie's.

At first she could not tell Mart. Somehow the very thought seemed to make their life so inevitably bound. Half expected that he would be so enraged at the thought of more poor health and uselessness—remembering her sister's continuous misery through all her childhood—that he would be more violent and insulting. Lettie was white and miserable herself those days. She had no strength or desire to quarrel and her very apathy seemed to arouse all the young, vigorous contrariness of Mart's nature, until it seemed as if he took a real delight in finding fault with each least thing.

Day after day it oppressed her. That sultry afternoon in June when she lay hot and limp on an old couch in the kitchen it seemed as if she had been cheated out of all youth and natural enjoyment. As if she had been utterly trapped. She had no strength to run away, and where could she have gone? No money, no real friends. Life at her sister's now, would be unbearable. Scores of memories crossed her mind at the mere thought. Babies screaming and untidy, fretful and unwashed—bottles sour and smelling—she fought down waves of nausea at the recollection. Was that to be her lot in life as well? To have to care for wretched, puny creatures . . . once, she remembered, out of that haze of horror—there had been a baby in the store—clean, firm, pink-cheeked, who had caught her eyes, and smiled at her in passing. Odd that a memory like that should strike her now. If only babies could be more like that—and then Lettie sat up very suddenly. One of those rare, clear flashes had shot all unbidden through her mind, and her eyes widened at the astonishing wonder of it. Why—what was there to prevent any baby she might some day have, from being pink and clean and healthy—if she took care to try and make it so.

If Mart noticed as the days went by, that Lettie's feet did not drag quite so heavily, that the meal table was neat and clean, and that she sat quietly, eyes distant instead of complaining, her voice, instead of querulous, preoccupied and absent, he made no sign. For Lettie, he had concluded by now, did not even interest him. She was a dismal failure as a wife; had no companionable qualities—not that he had even thought of that, at first—but since, through his own folly, he had brought it on himself, he must endure her presence as well as he was able. For marriage to him, was something inviolate.

Perhaps that was the reason Mart, coming up the steps one evening, automatically stooped to pick up some small stitchery that Lettie had dropped; and then had held it in his hands, half frowning. "Lettie—I guess this doesn't mean—does it?" His voice was slow and rather hesitant as his eyes met hers. But Lettie, in a swift frenzy of self consciousness snatched the garment away, springing to her feet. "Don't you interfere with me!" quite fiercely. He stared, almost uncomprehending. "Me! Why not! I guess I . . ." his continued scrutiny was so long and silent that she grew hotly uncomfortable. "Well!" and she backed up defensively. "It's true enough then. I guess that's just one more worry to your life!"

"Yes?" And all at once the odd hesitance of his stare was gone. It remained only hard and set. "I guess the idea of being a bit useful doesn't appeal to you much."

So perhaps, although the fault was largely hers, it was not wholly to be wondered at when Lettie picked up her work, and with the remark that she was going to bed, left the room. But perhaps the soreness of her heart as she lay alone in the darkness, was more surprising. For she had not remotely expected Mart to be reasonable or understanding. She had expected annoyance and savage argument—and yet his mere hard bitterness had stung more than she would have thought was possible. The thought that he measured her only in terms of usefulness—and that this, since it was useful, had received an almost startled share of his grudging attention. Curiously enough she knew then that she would have preferred real anger or contempt—somehow she could have cherished the thought of what was to be hers more closely then. But now—she lay awake, hot and resentful, long after Mart had stretched his long limbs silently beside her, and was breathing deeply.

Next morning as Lettie sat down to her breakfast, she was astonished to see Mart enter the kitchen and quite solemnly set down a rich glass of cream beside her plate—cream that was precious and rarely used within. So astonished that her eyes were wide as her glance met his.

"What's that for?" Perhaps her voice was unusually abrupt, for a deeper colour crept beneath the clear tan of his cheeks. "Well!" after a rather awkward silence. "I guess maybe you ought to feed a bit more. You're pretty thin . . . and . . . " he stumbled on rather hastily. "And—it'd be as well to have a healthy kid . . ."

"But . . . Mart . . ." and just for that one moment her rising anger was forgotten at the queer, flushed seriousness of his face; some look that she had never seen before.. "Do you mean you want it—yourself—apart from it just being something useful for me to do?"

"Want it!" In a sudden, unaccustomed nervousness he struck his fist on the table so that all the dishes jangled sharply. "Why wouldn't I want a kid—all my own—anyway!" Only, as it happened, it was not until that very moment that Mart had even as much suspected that he did, and it had merely been some strange, rough pity for Lettie's pale, thin weakness that had prompted his attention.

But Lettie could not know that. She was only aware of a wretched tide of anger—first at the way Mart had set that cream before her, solidly and flatly, as if she were one of his barnyard beasts, to be treated unemotionally for the time being with special care—and all at once a blaze of sheer fury and jealousy caught her. To think that Mart should want her child, and look like that about it . . . She stood up swiftly, and pushed the glass so violently that the contents half spilled over the table. "I don't want your fine feeding!" hotly. "Ugh!" and she shuddered with a real enough distaste. "The very look of it makes me sick!"

Mart stood a moment in stubborn silence. "Oh, well, if you want to be silly!" curtly, and with a faint shrug of the shoulders turned and left her standing there.

Only, through the hot, almost reasonless anger that had flared in both their undisciplined young beings, there had been a vague, hardly conscious sense that, somehow, one other moment had passed them by—a moment that might so easily have turned out very differently—and yet, both being what they were, could not have turned out any other way.

Then, for a little while, all Lettie's energies were

concentrated on resenting Mart. Resenting his silence, his lack of interest, and even, foolishly, the very fact that he was in the house at all. Hating to think that he had any claim over the small life to come—so that the temporary quiescence of her soul was gone, and she was restless, despondent and querulous again. Perhaps if she had known some of the neighbouring women things might have been better—but they had known no welcome ever at the Matthews home, and hesitated now. Besides, as they had heard—'a cheap, trashy girl from one of the stores'—the sort that Mart would pick— 'she'll want nothing from us.' So that Lettie, in all her youth and inexperience, was left alone to face a responsibility she could not be expected to know how to handle—and her only companion a youth, taciturn and stubborn, who knew no better himself how to meet the circumstances that had brought and bound their lives together.

And so, perhaps it almost happened that that brighter gleam which had come to Lettie's life was lost. Almost—and it would have been so easy to have slipped back into the slovenly unloveliness which had surrounded her since childhood, and which had been a part of the Matthews farm itself. Almost—except for the astonishing fact that somewhere far beneath all Lettie's silliness and shallowness and disconcent was an almost submerged sense of beauty and commonsense—qualities that might so easily have lain dormant all her life. Beauty—that through all her misery and sickness had made her remember that other pink cheeked baby she had seen—and common-sense that somehow, almost against her will, drove her back into the warm sunlight and the open air, and that made her eat, for the first time in her life, with conscious care. There was no one to tell her —and it was all the more surprising when almost imperceptibly a smooth tan and colour replaced the wan wretchedness of her face, and her arms grew firm and round where they before had been only limp, fleshless sticks. Many things, in those long solitary days while Mart was busy outside, came to her that she had not known. That there could be an elemental pleasure in keeping things clean and shining—and once when she found some old, dusty packets of flower seeds in the cupboard, an odd thrill caught her heart—so that in the days that followed she slowly managed to clear a tiny patch about the weed grown front steps, and plant several small, neat rows. She caught Mart staring at her once as she struggled there, and unwelcome colour filled her face—to think that he should catch her doing something 'useful' like that. But his glance held no apparent interest. "Do you want me to turn that ground?" he asked with sudden abruptness. "You!" She straightened sharply. "I thought you liked to see me being useful!" and found herself unaccountably hot and trembling in that moment. His lips tightened. "Sure I do," and flung back over his shoulder as he re-entered the house. "Only there's no sense in doing fool garden work in the daytime just now. is there? It's too late for seeds, anyway."

Fool garden work! Nor was it she of whom he was thinking. She knew that well enough. But somehow all her simple pleasure in the seeds was gone, and a little later she went indoors rather listlessly. It was Mart himself a few days later, who remarked rather caustically that she couldn't stick at anything, could she, and were even a few seeds too much for her. Lettie for the moment was so astounded at this obvious injustice that she stood stock still before the sink, two plates in hand, and then swung around with a stamp of her foot, so swiftly that he was startled. "Mart Matthews!" hotly. "What's the use of doing anything around this house when all you want's a pig-sty—and enough to eat. I'm just fed up with it all!"

While Mart, who might have made a dozen biting retorts and who, only a few weeks ago might have been tempted to half shake the life out of her, met her eyes sharply with a strange, surprised darkening of his own. "But Lettie . . ." and finally, there was a touch of that same hesitance that had seized him once or twice before. "You . . . didn't want to make things more decent around here—for my benefit—did you?"

For a moment Lettie's own glance was startled. She had caught a glimpse of something in his face that was not hard or indifferent—something which, had she been able to understand—spoke more of loneliness than anything else. But it was an expression so fleeting, that the next instant it was only the Mart of whom she was more than a little afraid, who stared at her. She tossed her head. "I should say I don't!"

A strange existence; for even their proximity and isolation from the world brought them no nearer. Yet their living together, for all that, must have taught them something. For Mart, however tired, never failed to clean himself before sitting down at table, and he continued to do the heavy work, uncomplainingly. Yet they would have scorned to admit that vaguely each was trying to struggle onwards to some still unseen end. For it was something, after all not easily defined, when they felt life had cheated them by giving them each other.

So the long summer days cooled into the rich beauty of the autumn, and into Lettie's face had stolen something of which no one, once knowing her, would have dreamed. Not peace—but some strange glow that spoke of health and cleanliness and order—and eyes that held in them a knowledge of the beauty of the golden fields and far hills about her. A restless glow perhaps, for there was always the thought of that small life to come in the depths of the winter—and that strange jealousy that drew and kept them far apart. It was all wrong—she knew that now. But it had gone too far, and there was nothing she alone could do.

Then all at once the neighbours seemed to discover strange things. That Lettie Matthews was no longer a cheap, shallow little schemer—but that she was a brown, rather appealing child with wide eyes and subdued voice—and so soon to be a mother—and that no woman had ever sought to help or give advice before. They found Mart Matthews instead of a mere slow, surly hulk of a lad, a straight, clean cut young fellow with a well kept house and farm, and with something alive and half frightened beneath the graveness of his eyes—and a wealth of kindness sprang about them both. It made it desperately hard; the offers of cradles and bathtubs—the warm assumption that they loved each other dearly; when neither of them had even known the meaning of real love at all.

Only one October evening Lettie unexpectedly came down into the kitchen, and found Mart standing by the small white cradle that she and Mrs. Adams had been working on that afternoon; awkwardly touching the small pink blankets that once had covered Tommy Adams, Junior. And she, a little embarrassed by the awkward defiance in his attitude as he sprang back, spoke out of an unexpected, quick desire to cover that confusion. "It's pretty, Mart, isn't it?"

"Why—sure . . ." but Mart was suddenly suspicious, and it must have been something born solely out of a confusion of thoughts within that made his retort so quick and savage. "Well—I don't see why I shouldn't want a kid of my own, anyway!"

"Well, Mart Matthews, I never said a thing about it!" and colour deep as his own filled her own face in that instant.

"Oh I know." He kicked at the floor with one hard boot, and burst out with defensive irritability. "I'm not a fool. You've never cared for anything . . . but that!" jerking his head towards the cradle. "And just because I want . . ." he stopped abruptly. "Oh I don't care. Do what you like!" with irrelevant unreasonableness that much later in the night, she spoke quite unexpectedly out of the darkness. "Mart—you didn't mean you wanted me to care—for you—did you?" and then had lain tense, with pounding heart. Whatever madness had prompted that query.

"No!" The answer came at once, quite fiercely, for Mart had been as wide awake as she. And then, after a prolonged silence, "I only married you because I wanted someone to . . . to be useful, yes . . ." with a hurried bitterness, as if he anticipated her thought. "So I'd hardly expect . . ." But he had not meant it quite like that—and in his blundering inability to express himself, he had only increased the soreness of her heart—and his own.

And finally, after weeks of interminable waiting it was December. Weeks in which Lettie's colour had paled with strain and lack of sunshine; and the outside ground was hard and frost bitten. Out of those weeks a diffident politeness, born of sheer necessity had grown between Mart and Lettie, and all arrangements had been made in the little hospital twenty miles away, and that she would stay with Mart's aunt in town a week or so before. It was settled that on the 12th, Mr. and Mrs. Harper, five miles beyond, who would be going into town in their closed car, would pick up Lettie on the way, with her belongings. So that it was not within the plan of things at all when Lettie woke her husband on the night of the 10th with a "Mart I think we'll have to go to town right now!"

O the two, Mart was the most frightened. He had not expected this. He sat up swiftly, and his face in the light of the lamp she held went queerly white. And then he was out of bed in a bound. "It's alright, Mart." Her voice was perfectly steady, as he fumbled almost blindly for his clothes. "I'm dressed, and everything's ready. There's some hot coffee, and your thick boots downstairs. Only . . ." with just a momentary apprehensive glance towards the window. "It's snowing . . . and I thought we'd better not be too long . . ."

Mart flung himself downstairs without a word, and into the shed where the old car stood in chill seclusion. Ten minutes later it was on the road outside, Lettie in rugs and Mart's heaviest sweaters in the front seat, and Mart himself, with lips tight set gripping the wheel.

That was a drive they would not soon forget. A bitter, driving wind, and snow that gathered on the glass until Mart could scarcely see a yard ahead. Wheels that despite their chains slipped wildly, and the engine roared and strained until it seemed inevitable that something mus give way.

And something did—for if any miracles were to be performed that night, it was not the car that did them. Only a mile or so away—a sudden gear change as the car slid in a rut on a sharp hill, and after one loud crack the engine raced impotently, and the wheels slipped backwards. Mart pulled up the brakes, and for the briefest instant sat with hands that clutched the steering wheel with vice-like grip.

"What is it Mart?" sharply.

"Axle I think", between set teeth. "Oh damn!" a moment later as he stood in the road getting his exact bearings. "Mart, won't it go at all?" Lettie leaned over, and he could just catch a glimpse of her pinched white face in the gloom. At this silence she herself was so momentarily still that in sudden fright he reached forward and felt for her arm. "Lettie, listen!" breathlessly. "I'll run to Simmons—it's only a mile on. They've got a phone. I'll get help . . . !" His very anxiety that she would scream and grow hysterical made his voice even unusually curt. But Lettie lost no time in hysterics, and almost before he knew it she was on the ground beside him. "No, don't to that." She spoke quickly. "Let's get back home. It can't be far. And then go on the horse, and phone."

"But good gosh, Lettie!" Although of course it was the most eminently sensible thing to do, there was utter consternation in his voice. "You can't walk!"

"I can, Mart. I'll have to!" Quite without thinking, she clutched his arm, and her voice was swift and urgent. "Mart, it's the only way, really. And I must move to keep warm."

And if they were not to forget the ride out, still less would the memory of that walk back escape them. Stumbling along through ever increasing swirling snow; and Lettie's grasp, light and even a little timid at first, grew heavier, and her breathing harsh and jerky. In Martin's heart was a terror he had never known before—to think that the girl he had married so carelessly, and who had suffered so much already—quite suddenly it seemed out of that dreadful night, he realized all that she must have suffered—should have to go through torments like this, because of him. He slipped his own strong young arm about her for support as he felt her stumble, and her footsteps falter. "You're sure you're alright, Lettie?" She must have sensed the torture that was in his voice, for she tried to straighten. "Yes, Mart." His grip tightened in silence and his eyes strained ahead—for they must be more than half way there—and if that courage he had always ignored, could keep her up a little longer . . . as he felt Lettie stumble more badly, he stopped short, and caught her unresisting in his arms, her head fell back against his shoulder. He just heard the muffled words "Mart . . . maybe it's our own punishment—for getting married without love!" He forged ahead, arms stiff with cold, and strain—but the perspiration pouring down his face as her words hammered dully through and through his brain. It was only as he laid her on the rumpled bed back in their home, that her eyes opened wide and comprehending, and her voice was faint and clear. "Mart—I hope—the baby will be alright, anyway—for you!" and just for one brief moment before he had to leave her there, on that mad race for aid, he dropped beside the bed, and his arms held her as they had never done before. "Lettie!" and it was some urgent cry from the very depths of his heart that spoke in that rough whisper. "I don't care about a thousand babies . . . it's you I want! I want you more than anything on earth . . . !"

At three o'clock next afternoon, the doctor and two farm wives were still in the room upstairs, and at half past four the former stepped down for a moment in the kitchen. "There's a fine boy up there," he spoke abruptly to Mart, who stopped his restless pacing to stand, utterly taut and still before him. "But, my lord, man, you should have known better than to let her out at all on such a night . . ." and then perhaps because he realized much of the youth and inexperience of them both, and because he had children himself their age who had never known a day's care in their lives, he dropped his hand more kindly on Mart's shoulder. "Never mind, son—you neither of you understood . . ." His voice grew grave. "It's pretty serious though . . ." and Mart's hand suddenly went out and clutched the older man's arm. "Doctor—for heaven's sake, don't let her go. Not now—not when I've always been so . . . I want to show her how I really care. Doctor, I'll do anything . . .!"

"I think . . ." and the Doctor's deep voice was gentle in that moment, "if anything will hold her, it will be the fact that you two do care for each other so much. That thought in itself, would always . . ." But Mart turned suddenly, and strode out of the kitchen door into the wintry gloom. "Our punishment—for getting married without love." Our punishment—if she went now, the bitterness of that could never leave his heart.

But late that evening, they let Mart into the upstairs bedroom, and he stood a moment staring down at the tiny red faced bundle in the cradle. Then the women left him there, looking down at that other face, almost as white as the pillows on which it lay. She smiled very faintly. "Do you like our son?"

Our son! Even while something of the wonder of that caught at his heart, there was no conscious thought at the moment of that tiny, red faced morsel. "Lettie!" his voice was very low and strained. "They—they think it was because we—loved—each other. These women said—it was because you had so much to live for . . ."

"Well, haven't I?" and there was something in the softness of her voice—in the faint glow of those tired eyes that met the almost desperate appeal in his own, that made Lettie in that moment nearly beautiful. "If you meant what you said last night . . .?"

"Meant it!" Just for an instant something seemed to break in Mart—and then, because he knew he must be very quiet, he knelt down and hid his face from sight. But one arm stole across the coverlet, and her fingers touched the bright gold hair that she had loved, despite herself, so many months.

But when Mart raised his head at length, and spoke, he touched a wistful chord in both their hearts. "Lettie—it's kind of good to think our kid will grow up in a happy home, where he's really wanted. If maybe we can teach him what we've had to learn ourselves . . ."

* * *

From such a marriage, nothing good or beautiful! No one who might have seen them then, could ever say that now.

# Zero Hour

## by Roderick Stuart Kennedy

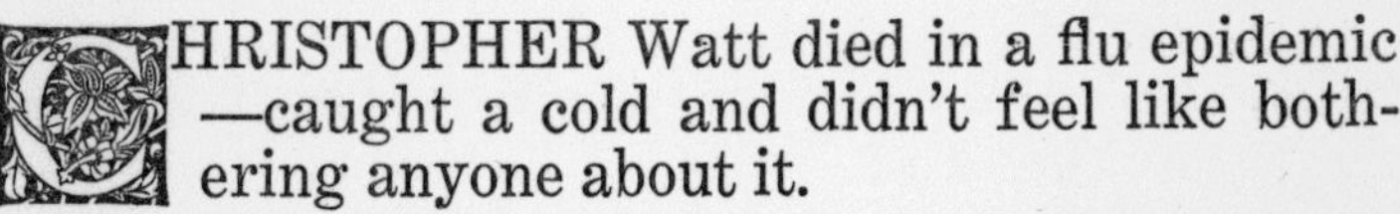

CHRISTOPHER Watt died in a flu epidemic —caught a cold and didn't feel like bothering anyone about it.

Mrs. Watt had him decently buried by one of the less expensive undertakers, and spoke of the virtues of "poor Christopher" in terms of becoming modesty. The name was rather a surprise to some of her friends, who had always heard of him —if at all, as C.W." If it had not been for the solemnity of the occasion some of them might have felt like smiling. Such an important name for such an unobtrusive little man!

The boys at the office did the regular thing and put up a dollar apiece for a wreath—you can't very well get out of it, but what with all these funerals and weddings——! Oh well! Sure, put me down for a buck.

There was no fuss. The local newspaper printed a brief obituary notice, but it was the kind that costs two dollars—regular card rates, in the Births, Marriages, and Deaths column. The one at the back of the paper among the Want Ads., with the stream line heading across the top of the page, "Star Want Ads. Bring Quick and Satisfactory Results."

Everything was very commonplace when Christopher died. Nobody was in the least excited.

But Christopher was excited! Very much so.

And it was a distinctly unpleasant excitement too. It wasn't the rushing darkness, or the sense of illimitable space and speed that he was worrying about. It wasn't the journey at all, it was the destination!

It was a subject he hadn't given much thought to when he was alive; but now he was dead—and he was giving it very serious thought.

What were his chances? For in spite of that sense of terrifying speed through a great emptiness, there was nothing to show whether he was going up or down.

He couldn't remember doing any very wicked things. He'd plugged away at his job, been reasonable with the wife, helped the occasional lame dog over a stile, stuck by his friends. He'd enlisted and gone through the war, but he'd never got beyond being a Private. Besides, he'd rather wanted to enlist, so that wouldn't bring him any credit; and come to think of it most of the things he was taking credit for had been ones that he'd wanted to do. Pure selfishness if you went to the bottom of it, and Christopher had an uncomfortable feeling that THEY would go to the bottom of it.

The thought gave him a nasty sinking feeling; and when you are on your way to—well, when you don't know where you are on your way to, a sinking feeling is the last kind you want.

Still he'd gone to church fairly often, that was something. But would he have gone if his wife hadn't taken him? Christopher groaned in spirit. No! He couldn't fool himself, he hadn't been a righteous man. Really good men showed it. Look at Mr. Wimpers, his neighbor; look at that fellow who'd spoken at the Forum—what was his name? —the man who wrote the syndicated sermonettes —men whose goodness was proved out of their own mouths—impressive, both of them, as he'd never been.

Deep in his soul he admitted that he never had been impressive like really good men. Even when lending somebody a helping hand, he'd never impressed himself that he was being good. He must lack something—force, that was it, and didn't it say somewhere that the Kingdom of Heaven was only to be taken by force? Something like that. A fat chance he'd have!

The awful, empty, rushing silence wore on his spirit. He began to get very frightened indeed.

If he couldn't impress himself, looking on the best side of things, he certainly couldn't fool THEM.

The other side wouldn't be overlooked either, when THEY looked up his record. Not on your life!

He'd voted against Prohibition, he'd gambled on horse races, half a dozen times at least, he hadn't loved his neighbors as himself—rather the contrary as far as that old—as far as Mr. Wimpers was concerned. Or was it your enemies that you had to love? If only he'd read his Bible oftener. Not that he had what you could call real enemies, but there were one or two people—and he disliked them still, that was the worst of it—sheer stubborn unrepentance!

His soul shrank. Look at what he'd done to some of those poor German enemies in the war! Couldn't help himself, true, but what about that trouble with his wife's brother? He could have helped that all right. Not that he'd actually done anything, but it was what you thought, not what you did that counted—and he'd thought a hell of a lot! Oh God, there he was swearing—and a blasphemy right on top of it! He was certainly canned now.

Gradually the dark emptiness pressed in on him. There was a deeper intensity to the silence. Something gigantic, eternal, was impending.

IT must be coming now. If only there were still time to repent; it was his one chance.

And Christopher Watt tried hard to repent—terribly hard. It was no good. The spirit was willing, but the flesh——! Ah, what a hopeless idea. He smiled sadly—the ghost of a smile. Trying to repent after you were dead! Too late, too late! That kind of repentance was no good—useless; there was no body to it.

The only possible chance was that THEY didn't

know everything about you, and that was really no chance at all for his soul was bared.

Christopher gave up hope. There was nothing for it but to say he was sorry and take his medicine.

And then space stood still, and there was no more darkness; and he looked at a huge open gate and a bearded figure with a great key who sat at a desk within, and at a vast crowd thronging at either side. And Christopher knew that it was Saint Peter whom he saw, and his soul shivered.

For a moment he waited, then Saint Peter looked up from his work, saw him standing there, and jumped to his feet. "Why, bless my soul, it's Christopher Watt!" And he came forward, laying his hand affectionately on Christopher's shoulder, with a wonderful smile which seemed to wrap him in a warmth of love and peace. He had never felt quite that way before, and two glistening drops crept from his eyes and fell—way, way down. And it chanced that they fell on the eyes of a quiet little man called Brown, who was having a rather tough time just then in one of the big cities below; and they rolled on out of his eyes, and down his cheeks—and Brown felt better.

Saint Peter was leading him gently within the gate. "Welcome, Christopher, a thousand times," he smiled, and waved away a record card proffered by one of the attendants. "Christopher Watt needs no card round here. Hardly!' And he turned to the crowd as if for confirmation.

Christopher could see that they were craning forward the better to see him. Murmurs came from all around. "It's Christopher Watt." "Sure, didn't you know? That's T H E Christopher Watt."

He felt awfully funny—like he used to feel when he was a little boy, coming into the warm, bright living room after the pitch black walk from the cold barn—sort of dazed—comfortably dazed, basking in the family friendliness after feeding all those animals that he was always doing things for without being taken any notice of.

Saint Peter was raising his hand. The murmuring ceased. "Is there anyone here from Mansion C?" he asked, and there was a slight movement in the crowd as three figures came forward. "Ah, Washington, always first when needed, eh? But you're in Section 4, aren't you? You received your full measure of fame on earth."

Suffused with comfortable contentment, Christopher could only wonder mildly at what was being said. It was like when Pa would read bits from the paper to the bright circle in the lamplight, things that he'd understand, but be too warm and sleepy to think about. But this wasn't Pa, of course, it was Saint Peter—there had been a picture of him in the old Church. Funny that everyone should be just like their pictures! He'd rather thought—and Washington!—the living image of the engraving in the old parlor, next to The Death of General Wolfe, and—gosh! that was Wolfe himself talking to Saint Peter now! Section 3? Why was Wolfe in Section 3! Received a portion of his fame before he died? How did that make any difference?

There seemed to be a lot of Sections in Mansion C. It must be a grand place to be—with people like that in it. And look—Edith Cavell!—that picture he'd had over his bureau ever since the war. His spirit leaped as Saint Peter beckoned. He was going to be allowed to speak to her!

"Let me introduce Christopher Watt, Miss Cavell. Yes, you know all about her, Christopher, that's why she's in Section 2—fame did come to her after death. Still you're next door, Edith, and it's no use waiting for any of those people in Section 1; they're always in the background somewhere, so you might take him along and show him the ropes, will you?"

Edith Cavell took Christopher Watt's hand to lead him away, when Saint Peter stopped them. "Just a minute, musn't forget the red tape."

He picked up the record card and started to read from it, reeling it off so quickly that Christopher couldn't understand a word until the very last, which rolled forth impressively for all of Heaven to hear.

". . . and did return to his regiment that night, sorely wounded, and report all that had seemed to him important namely and to wit, the loss of the rest of the detachment. And that he did make no mention, then or thereafter, of any of the aforementioned deeds of heroism and self sacrifice. Wherefore be it known that Christopher Watt shall be, and is hereby allotted to Mansion C, FOR GREAT BATTLE HEROES, and to Section 1 thereof, FOR THOSE WHOM FAME PASSED BY."

# The Gun Fighter

by Frederick B. Watt

WRIGLEY, the village philosopher, had more than once declared: "It will take a large-sized explosion to jar Tom Higgs loose from the job of town policeman." Wrigley was right.

It was a large-sized explosion—that is as explosions go in the town of Lancet. It was sufficiently large to blow the door off the vault of the Grain Growers' Bank and wake up eight hundred and seventy-three of the town's fifteen hundred inhabitants.

The explosion occurred at 3.16 on a nippy September morning. As a matter of fact Tom Higgs had been awake since 3.14 when McGillivray, the telegraph operator, had banged lustily on the door of the constable's two-roomed shack. Tom had shifted his sixty-one year old bones wearily out of his cot and mildly enquired, "What's the fuss?"

"God knows," snapped the young operator, "but I think something's wrong at the bank and I'm darn sure something's wrong with my wire. I've been cut off for fifteen minutes. I was walking up to the telephone office when I noticed a big car in front of the Grain Growers' Bank. It seemed to me the bank door was open. The phone wire's dead, too. Cut, I'll bet."

Tom Higgs was wide awake now.

"Bless my soul," he said, drawing on his trousers and reaching for the antiquated revolver that had been a thing of reverence and fear to the youngsters of the village for the past twenty years. Tom, it was said, had killed three Mexican bandits with it in his young days.

It was as the constable and the operator were hurriedly walking down the main street towards the bank building, that the explosion took place. A puff of smoke shot from the open bank door, a window pane tinkled to the wooden sidewalk and two of three men who were hugging the wall of the building plunged into the reeking room. The third member of the party remained leaning casually on the front fender of the big touring car that stood at the curb.

With dignity, almost pomposity, the constable stalked towards the watcher, swinging the big pistol carelessly at his side.

"Say, young fellow——" he exclaimed when he was about thirty paces from the car.

"Shut up, Dad, and clear out before you get

hurt," ordered the stranger, flourishing an automatic.

The constable raised his ancient weapon. A spurt of flame shot from the bandit's gun and Tom Higgs' hat was snatched from his head. Stubbornly he pulled at the trigger of the big revolver but there was no report. Revolvers cannot be left lying around unused for twenty years without getting somewhat rusty. The telegraphist jerked Tom back into the shelter of a doorway as a second bullet from the man by the car whistled past.

"I can't get it to go off," wailed Tom, nursing his useless fire-arm with withered fingers.

One of the men in the bank had appeared and had thrust something into the back seat of the car by the time young Winthrop, the insurance agent, appeared around the corner, clad in garish pyjamas and armed with a shot gun. The bandit sentinel opened fire on sight and his second shot dropped the audacious townsman with a bullet in his leg. Winthrop answered the gunman from where he lay and the double charge of bird-shot found a target in his enemy's face. The stricken gunman staggered backward, his hands to his riddled features. Screaming like a madman, he feel into his companion's arms and was promptly thrown into the car. The third man had appeared by this time and had jumped to the wheel. There was a grinding roar as the engine took hold. At 3.18 all that remained to testify to the fact that the town had been visited was a looted safe, a wounded insurance broker sitting cursing at the street-corner, a mild-eyed constable complaining about a gun that wouldn't go off, and a long trail of dust stretching in the direction of the international boundary.

At 2.30 the main street was filled with wildly excited townspeople and the air rang with innumerable questions. At 3.25, while the fumes of the explosion still hung heavily around the shattered vault, it was apparent that Tom Higgs had been jarred loose from his job.

* * *

Tom had always know the day would come when he would be discredited but the occasion had been so long delayed that a feeling of security had come over him. When the blow arrived it shook him badly.

For twenty years he had been everything the town policeman of Lancet should have been. He had been a terror to the children who stayed out after the nine o'clock curfew had tolled from the combination civic block, police headquarters and fire-station. He had always let it be known when he intended to visit the social club over the Chinese restaurant—with the result that there wasn't a single poker chip in sight when he arrived. He had religiously met the daily (except Sundays) train and kept a wary eye open for the slick city crooks who might, but never did, choose the town as their scene of operations.

Once a farmer had become insane on his homestead three miles from town and had killed his wife. Tom Higgs had been called for although the crime had been committeed outside his territory. He had been seriously thinking of resigning when Constable Clawson of the Provincial Police, a lean, clean-shaven, lantern-jawed young official, rode in upon the scene and took the burden from the quaking shoulders of old Tom. That had been the only disturbing incident in his whole tenure of office and in the ten years that had elapsed since that unpleasant episode he had been allowed to enforce the curfew law, meet the trains and hold down a chair in the Commercial Hotel "rotunda" without interruption. He had become as much a part of the sleepy life of the town as the daily (except Sundays) train or the long, straight line of white highway that ran to the American border.

The Lancet town council, at least the younger members of it, had realized that Tom was getting too old for the job but they, too, disliked a jog in the old order of things and they were quite prepared to pay the constable his meagre salary until he should pass out of the picture. Then perhaps some of the young fellows, who had been arguing that the office required an aggressive man, could have their innings.

But the nitro-glycerine that blew open the vault door in the Grain Growers' Bank disturbed the easy-going atmosphere of Lancet tremendously. The council met the next day, Tom Higgs was relieved of his duties and the red-faced son of Lancet's leading butcher replaced him. They made it as easy as they could for the deposed official, expressing their admiration for his courage and his long years of service. His demotion, they said, was not on account of the robbery but was a step that they had intended taking after his sixtieth birthday. Sixty, they figured, marked the end of a policeman's period of usefulness.

The victim saw the crash coming. He knew that he was done for when the council brought an end to the enquiry and asked him to step outside while they arrived at some decision. He didn't wait around but walked stiffly to his shack, two dusty blocks away. His few belongings he carefully packed into a couple of weather-beaten trunks. He took down the ancient pistol from the nail on the wall and eyed it sadly, accusingly.

"I wonder if you ever did work?" he demanded. A vision rose before him of the sleek Jewish second-hand dealer in the city who had sold it to him at an unbelievably low price the day he set out to apply for the job in Lancet twenty years before.

"Well, I'm sort of glad you didn't go off," he concluded forgivingly. "You sure would have made an awful bang and probably kicked my fingers off."

He wanted to get out of town that night. He had no place to go but he was a proud old man in his way and he couldn't bear the thought of the sympathy he would receive from the older people in the village—and the jeers from the youngsters as they ignored the curfew bell and exulted in the fact that his tyrannical reign had come to a close. Grimly he walked to the ramshackle stable at the rear of his shack and hitched his two decrepit cayuses to a rickety farm wagon. Seated on his meagre worldly possessions he rattled down the main street and drew up in front of the town hall, ignoring the inquisitive glances of his fellow townsmen.

"I'm sorry, Tom," said the reeve, "but we can't pay you today. The bank will have a new supply of money in tomorrow, though. Better go back to your shack tonight, there's no hurry about you getting out. Krauss isn't going to live there, anyway. He's going to keep staying at his father's house."

"No thanks," answered the ex-constable haughtily. "I guess I can camp on the prairie. I've done it enough in my time."

Twenty years of almost constant reminiscing on those mythical days of pioneering had pretty nearly convinced Tom that they had actually existed.

Not until he had reached a meadow outside the town did the charioteer pull up his snorting chargers, almost upsetting the cart in the process. Ah, this was life; the old life; the careless, unfettered life that had become so dear in an uncontrolled imagination. True, it took the best part of his box of matches to start his camp-fire without paper but it was such a brave, friendly blaze when once it took hold. It robbed the bleak sunset of its spirit of depression; it deprived the crisp Autumn dusk of its ability to chill old bones.

An hour later, however, lying beneath the cold stars and a couple of badly-holed horse blankets, he appreciated that the unroofed prairie was a dwelling place for only young men or those who had become hardened in youth.

He was still shaken with spasmodic outbreaks of shivering when he drew his wages that morning. Dr. Yarkes, one of his cronies, regarding him suspiciously as he emerged from the reeve's office.

"Leaving us already?" he asked with professional joviality, glancing at the horses and the wagon.

Tom Higgs nodded, refusing to trust his quavering voice.

"Better drop into the office and have a snort," suggested the doctor. "You look as though you could stand one."

"I'm all right," protested Tom weakly. "Just a touch of fever I picked up in Mexico."

Yerkes repressed a smile.

"Just for old time's sake," urged.

The deposed official surrendered. The thought of the hot liquid stinging its way through his half-frozen body and dulling the edges of the thousand icy swords that stabbed him, was too much to resist.

Tom Higgs was still in town at lunch time. He had at no time been a heavy drinker but the doctor's Scotch had proven such a boon that the bottle had been visited more than once—considerably more than once. When Yerkes suggested their lunching together at the Chinese cafe Tom was positively enthusiastic about it. He was still there at suppertime.

After supper he slumped, though, and gradually arrived at that stage which is usually the final destination of an unaccustomed drinker. He became sorry for himself. For a considerable time he sat in brooding silence while his companions, who were no longer dependent on him for amusement, continued to make merry. Finally he rose theatrically from his chair and surveyed his glowing audience with the eye of a martyr. His gaunt length swayed stiffly, like a brittle reed threatening to snap in a gust of wind.

"Men," he said—and his high pitched voice became almost sonorous for an instant—"I'm leaving you. There's plenty of fellows who will say, 'Well, there's the last of poor ol' Tom Higgs', when I cross the town limits. But they'll be wrong. You can't keep a good guy down. As the poet said, 'My bloody head is unbowed.' The day will come when this same bunch of fossils on the town council will be begging me to come back and keep order in this neck of the woods. They'll be callin' for Tom Higgs, Indian gunfighter!"
He accompanied the last defiant sentence with a startling movement of his hand beneath his coat and without warning, the gathering found the immense pistol flourishing in their faces. Doc Yerkes, leaning back in his chair, was so taken by surprise that he crashed over on his shoulders. His companions hurriedly ducked beneath the table. Tom, well satisfied with the effect he had created, stalked to the door where he stood swaying for a moment.

"Good-bye men," he croaked. "Just you remember what I've said."

His team was still in front of the office. Someone had possessed consideration enough to throw on their blankets and give them some hay and water. They were stiff and cold, though. and had almost as much difficulty in getting started as Doc Yerkes' 1916 Ford. Tom finally whipped them into a jog trot and, standing as tense as the popular picture of Ben Hur, he clattered down the road that led to the border. He didn't know where he was going and he didn't much care. The whisky was still warm within him.

At the edge of the town he stopped for a moment and made a sweeping bow to the little cluster of lights behind him. The effort almost threw him off the wagon and he regained his balance only just in time.

"Tom Higgs, you're a drunken old fool," he reprimanded himself with a childish chuckle.

A moment later he was standing on his dignity.

"You're nothing of the sort," he corrected. "You're a darn good fellow—too darn good for those grandmothers on the Lancet council. You're the best constable and the best Indian fighter that ever worked this side of the border. Curse 'em all."

Had he been sober he would have blushed at the language he was using.

On and on the cayuses jogged down the trail, showing about as much enthusiasm as though they were headed for the bone-yard, where they belonged. On and on raved the intoxicated Tom Higgs that had never existed outside the realms of fiction and swinging his formidable but harmless revolver with the abandon of a child with a new toy. Far behind the distant glow of a motor car's headlights drifted along the back trail like a huge butterfly and occasionally there came the muffled roar of a racing engine, as though the sleeping earth was snoring. But they failed to attract the notice of old Tom. He wasn't even aware that he was on a particularly dangerous bit of road, a long, straight stretch of "fill" over some boggy land.

"I'm Tom Higgs, Indian fighter!" he declared loudly, pointing a menacing weapon at the disinterested stars.

The roar of the engine had grown louder and as the car made a turn in the road and started down the long half-mile of "fill" the headlights shone directly on the man in the wagon. Still he was unperturbed. At three or four hundred yards the powerful beams made him visible to the men in the car and the long note of a siren shrieked out. The automobile didn't attempt to let up in its wild careening, however.

"Aw, go to the devil," growled Tom Higgs, blinking into the glare and twirling the revolver around his trigger finger as he had once seen a man do in the movies. "Who d'you think you are that you can hoot me off the centre of the road?"

On rushed the car. It was quite apparent that it would not be able to pass the cayuses as long as the wagon held the crown of the trail but the ex-constable possessed the stubbornness born of the best part of a bottle of whisky.

"Who are you to hoot at me? D'you know who I am? I'm——"

The car leaped at him out of the murk, heading straight for the wagon. At the last moment it made an effort to swing to one side. There was a terrific crash and the world ceased to hold any interest for Tom Higgs.

When he came to it was morning and he was in

the Lancet community hospital. He realized this fact as he opened his eyes and met the sympathetic gaze of Miss Giles, the matron. He moved his head to one side and an agonizing pang shot across his temples, causing him to wince and lie still. Had he been a more experienced drinker he would have immediately recognized the symptoms of a "morning after" headache but as it was he pictured his scalp as being broken in a dozen pieces.

"Will I live?" he asked the nurse weakly.

"Certainly," she reassured him, 'but Dr. Yerkes says you're to sleep as long as you can."

Feeling as he did, Tom was of the opinion that D. Yekes knew his business. He did his best to live up to the order. In a few moments, without asking any more questions, he dozed off. He awoke at noon but was still miserable and tired. He rolled over and failed to show any signs of life until supper time. It was then that he suddenly discovered he was exceedingly hungrey and that his head was rapidly coming down to its normal size. Raising himself on his elbows he found himself beneath the kindly stare of Dr. Yerkes.

"Well, howsaboy?" asked the physician. "Ready to see people?"

"Sure, provided they bring some food with 'em," answered Tom between gasps, raising his creaky carcass with a painful effort.

"The reeve's outside," said the doctor. "He's come with a request from the council asking you to take on your old job at an increased salary."

"Aw, lay off," pleaded the ex-constable, "and tell me who hit me."

"Here, read this," ordered Yerkes exultantly, thrusting a copy of the morning paper from the city into Tom's lean hands.

This is what he saw:

" 'Bad' Morgan, Chicago gunman, was killed and Jerry Ripper, his pal, fatally injured shortly before midnight on Tuesday following the looting of the Grain Growers' Bank at Lancet, a small farming town near the American border on the A. B. & X. Railway. The bandits had succeeded in making their escape from Lancet, having terrorized Constable Krauss and a band of townsmen who attempted to drive them from the bank, but at a point seven miles south of the village they were intercepted by Tom Higgs, who had been relieved of his position as constable two days previous.

"Higgs, suspecting that something unusual had occurred, threw the wagon he was driving across the road and drew his revolver. The desperate criminals drove straight at him but he stood his ground. The car hit the wagon a glancing blow, the vehicles being thrown one to either side of the road. Higgs' wagon was demolished and he was hurled into a clump of willows. He was rendered unconscious but is reported to be resting easily this morning, suffering mainly from shock.

"The bandit's car struck a telephone post and turned over. Morgan was thrown through the wind-shield and struck his head against the pole, dying instantly. Ripper, who was driving, was jambed beneath the steering wheel and was badly crushed when pinned beneath the wreackage. He was taken to the Lancet hospital where he died at an early hour his morning.

"Ripper, hardened criminal though he was, paid a glowing tribute on his death-bed to the man who had brought him to book for his many offences against society. Higgs, he said, had awaited the charge of the speeding automobile with the greatest courage, flourishing his revolver and shouting at the bandits to stop until the moment the crash occurred.

"He also confessed that he and his companions were the same men who raided the Lancet bank early Sunday morning. They had figured that a sudden return would catch the town off its guard. He admitted that a third accomplice, who had been with them in the first robbery, had been rendered blind by a charge of bird-shot. The gang was credited with a full dozen border raids.

"Constable Krauss who refused to face the menacing guns of the outlows, has resigned and it is anticipated that the former official will be urged to return to his post. Tom Higgs, who will receive a handsome cash reward from the Banker's Association, is a well known character in the West. He was a famous gun fighter in his youth."

# Instead of the Thorn

## by Frances Beatrice Taylor

"SIN," said Uncle Christopher, "is a queer thing!"

He eased himself a little in the narrow confines of the wooden pillory, and wriggled his toes, which were growing stiff.

"And there is this, too," Uncle Christopher said. "They make far too much ado about it in this place."

He addressed himself seriously to a small wren which poised on a tiny swaying branch above him, watched him with warily cocked head and bright, intent eye.

"Now you, my littling, for all the meek look of you, only an hour agone were helping yourself to your neighbor's supper as like as not." He sighed. "Can you tell me, littling, why a neighbor's supper is so much sweeter than our own?"

"This particular place where I now am is damnably uncomfortable," he added decisively. But the wren flipped an impudent tail at him and was off.

The summer silence closed in, drowsing around him. He was a sorry figure enough, his wrists tethered, his ankles in the awkward wooden frame, the grass green and thick about him, and the little, kindly winds ruffling the fine silver of his hair. Yet there was an odd mixture of dignity and merriment about him, for all his plight.

"It's little enough breath they leave a man, what with their rough handling," he grumbled, "but enough maybe for a stave or two."

He began to sing, his voice, rich and tuneful, rolling out over the quiet green.

"Day of wrath, oh day of mourning!" shouted Uncle Christopher with a will. But he broke off with an exclamation of delight entirely unconnected with the letter or spirit of the song.

"By my faith!" cried Uncle Christopher, "If it is not my little Glorianna, come to comfort her old one in his dire extremity."

The girl stood beside him and laid a hand, swift and tender on his silver hair.

"Uncle Christopher, dear Uncle Christopher, you should not be here!"

"By the gods I should not!" he agreed. "Would it be asking your Loveliness too much to fetch the keys from your father's house and unfasten this contraption," he suggested hopefully.

The girl shook her head. "The keys are always with him," she said sadly.

"Like the poor," Uncle Christopher said. "But

in truth," he added, "it would be a sorry trick to play on the village folk. They will be wanting an evening of sport out of an old man in the stocks. Were it not market day, they would have been here ere this. Now, could I cheat them of their fun?"

"I cannot bear that you should be here thus, and they reviling you," the girl cried bitterly.

"Nay, child, they are decent folk enough, and kind, and merry, if my good brother would let them be so. A strange man, your father, Glorianna!"

She looked startled. "We must not say that," she reproved him. "He is a minister of God. And he must rebuke sin."

"Maybe, maybe," Uncle Christopher agreed. "But he finds a deal of sin where none is meant."

"The world is full of sin, and corruption," the girl said, the words rounded queerly in the young, pliant voice. "The wrath of God is upon it."

"And lady-smocks all silver white
And cuckoo buds of yellow hue,
Do paint the meadows with delight—"

Uncle Christopher hummed irrelevantly.

"What are those words, Uncle Christopher?" the girl asked.

"You'll not find them in the Book of Books," her uncle said. "They were writ by a lad called Will Shakespeare, and having little learning in books, I got them from a priest in Rome that I met once in a travelling way over on the road beyond Marseilles."

"Nay, Uncle" the girl's voice was suddenly tearful. "We idle here, and yet time passes and punishment is coming upon you."

"My father is filled with terrible anger. And my lord has returned, and is at the Great House, and my father says that he shall mete out punishment to you, since it was on his lands you went thieving."

"Tush, a rabbit and a stoat or two!" Uncle Christopher dismissed the theft with a twist of his handsome lip. "This fine gentleman at the Great House? They say he is as great a sinner as myself."

"My father says there is naught but sin in him; that his eye blighteth whatsoever it looks upon," the girl said earnestly.

"A most unpleasant fellow, then," murmured Uncle Christopher. "Please God he looks the other way when he passes judgment on me."

"But he will put you in prison, Uncle Christopher; maybe he will even send you far away, over the sea." Her voice trembled.

The old man looked at her gently. "Do not weep, my pretty one. He will not be so harsh for so small an offence. Being himself a sinner. Only your father is so stern. Are you afraid of your father, Clorianna?"

"When I anger him; his anger is terrible. He has forbidden me to hearken when you call me that strange name."

"Glorianna, Glorianna—" Uncle Christopher turned the syllables delicately on his tongue. "And for what did the good God give you a mane of gold, blazing like the beech trees in October, if you were not to be called Glorianna? What name else could I call you by?"

"'My name is Abigail," the girl said primly.

"Abigail!" Uncle Christopher scoffed. "A pettifogging name, and no beauty in it. Nay, you are Glorianna. Queen of faery, and your hair is burnished like the sun, and your eyes are deep purple like the pansies, and you are altogether lovely."

"Listen to the Song of Songs, which is Solomon's," he added suddenly. " 'Behold thou art fair, my love, behold thou art fair!' A mighty judge of womenkind, Solomon!"

"You do jest on God's holy word," Abigail said. "And I am afraid for you—dear Uncle Christopher—why are you so great a sinner?"

"There are but two things a man may not be forgiven of God," Uncle Christopher said. "Riding hard to the place where danger is not, and bringing evil on little children and on the small creatures of the wood. Save, of course, the rabbits and maybe a stoat or two," he sighed.

"My father is good," Abigail said, and sighed.

"Is he so good then?" her uncle asked. "I could wish that his goodness might be turned to making this place more comfortable, since I am like to be his guest here until the morning."

"And after that you must go before my lord, and he will set heavy punishment upon you, and you will go away, and I will see you no more."

"Then, pretty one, plead with your good father for me."

"He would not hearken," the girl said sorrowfully. "He is angered at me, indeed, and did he know that I came to you here, his anger would be greater. What heed would he pay to my prayer?"

"He was never one to be moved by beauty," Uncle Christopher admitted. "I doubt there is another man in the country who could look on you, and not grant your prayer."

The girl caught her breath with a sudden resolve.

"Should you mind so much, going to prison?" she asked very low.

Uncle Christopher moved his fingers and toes an inch, deprecatingly. The gesture was as though he had puffed away an unimportant something.

"A man must taste of life at the full," he said easily. "But I could wish it might not be in high summer," he added.

Abigail stood looking down at him for a moment, her eyes dark with some strange, unuttered pain.

"Uncle Christopher, I—I love you," she stammered. She bent quickly and pulled a spray of clover, richly headed in purple, from the lush grass at her feet and thrust the bloom into his hand. Then she turned and went on quick feet along the path.

Uncle Christopher, left alone, stirred the scented flower with stiff fingers. He twisted his shoulders and made a grimace of pain. Then he smiled.

"And here am I, sitting with a piece of clover in me hand, and all the world going by!" he said.

Abigail ran quickly, her small, rough shoes ruffling the dust in the lane. The soft sounds of the summer afternoon were all around her. There were blackberries in the hedge and a wild rose, last remnant of the bannered army which stormed the lanes a week or so ago. The leaves of the poplar trees by the old mill whispered, turning to show an edge of silver that presaged rain.

In the grim, grey-fronted house with its blind unlovely eyes, the house from which Parson Furnaby dispensed his stern justice and sought erring souls for God, the evening tasks waited to be done. She tied a spotless apron over the sombre gown, and began to lay the table for the simple supper, fetching milk and butter from the little stone walled dairy in the hillside, back of the house.

The mail was ready when her father and mother came in, and she stood behind her chair waiting. Richard Furnaby, like his brother, was a tall man, and broad but he was thin to emaciation, and his shoulders were bent a little, as if with some unseen burden. Abigail had her eyes from him, deep violet, washed in with the dark bands of heavy lashes but his had narrowed as if he gazed always into some strange, intangible and terrifying distance. His mouth, with its thinly-cut beautiful lips, was closely folded.

She tried to look at her mother, but Mrs. Furnaby's eyes were on her plate. Once she reprimanded the girl for her neglected food, and Abigail tried again to eat.

Her father spoke. His voice destined for rich

tones, had thinned and he uttered his words with a cold precision that Abigail dreaded. She knew her father in all his moods, and most she feared the ice cold grip of his justice, a justice that knew no compromise, no half measures. Sometimes, shaken with a fire of oratory, he pronounced the wrath of God, painting vivid, gleaming, terrible pictures. But she was not so much afraid of him, then, as now, when he was like the God he served, implacably just, unalterably vengeful.

When the meal was over, and she rose to set the place to rights again, he stopped her. His voice was cold; only his eyes were like flames of wrath.

"You visited my brother, in the place where I had meted out punishment to him," he said slowly. "You have brought shame upon us, and for this I have said that you shall not enter the house of God until I have a sign that His anger is appeased."

The girl gave a little cry, cowering as though he had struck her. But he strode past her to the door, then, turning, raised a hand.

"Do you sin so again, you go from this house also, and forever," he said.

Uncle Christopher would have laughed. "He was always one for play-acting, for all he said all play-folk were sinners," he told her once. But she saw nothing amusing nor even pitiful in her father's anger. To her, it was as great, as terrible, almost, as the wrath of God.

Her mother helped her with the simple household tasks, but she gave her no word of comfort. Sometimes it seemed to Agibail that all life in her mother had died under great consuming thought like a flame that burned her through and through. When the work was done, Mrs. Furnaby walked across the narrow flagged kitchen, where the last light still lingered in fragrant, dusty rays. She did not look at Abigail, as she tied the grey bonnet under her chin. Her eyes were cold, but the girl was so shaken by the fierceness of her own resolve that tonight she felt none of the rack that sometimes pierced her with so sharp a pain.

When they were gone, and there was only the ticking of the clock and the soft sound of the evening about her, she put on the little grey bonnet that was like her mother's and the narrow ugly grey cloak. Between the sharp rims of the bonnet the lovely face was white and the eyes dark with fear. But she went out through the narrow garden, where the neat rows of cabbages and lentils were her task, and through the gate into the pasture meadow. The parsonage where the Furnabys lived, was on a corner of the Great House lands; it was a poor place enough but Parson Furnaby paid rent meticulously to my lord's agent. He would have no traffic with the unbeliever.

Beyond the meadow lay the park, but the long avenue leading to the house was on the farther side There was a shorter way, though; Abigail knew it, for once, when they had first come to the village, she had wandered there. She had not forgotten the sharp reprimand the thoughtless act had brought from her father. She had never seen my lord; few in the village had, though his name and his wrongdoing were a byword. He had inherited the place from a distant relative, and only once or twice had visited it, though, through his agents he meted out a sort of justice to the villagers, mostly his tenantry.

All this Abigail knew. The rest—the long record of sins credited to the master of the Great House, she only guessed. Her father had hinted at them, darkly. The villagers, under his stern influence shunned the park and she herself had never seen the house. She knew the thing she must do, and in spite of the fear that gripped her, she went on. In the park, the great trees drew in, folding her in a soft, fictitious darkness for the sun was still high in the west though the shadows were longer in the meadows and the droning of the afternoon had turned to the deeper, more mysterious sounds of evening.

She came out on a little terrace above the park, on grass that was soft and thick as velvet under her feet. Beyond, on a stone parapet a peacock stood, his fan dropped, the late night on his jewelled head. Against the grey wall, the color stabbed her like a rapier. Below him roses grew in a walled garden. From where she stood she could see the flowers hanging heavy heads in the afterglow. From the park beyond, the twilight advanced on cool, noiseless feet and even while she watched, the color began to fade softly from the roses, drawn into that tender, protecting darkness.

From the long windows of the house, narrow threads of mellow light came out on the grass. She could see into the room, the dining-hall, it must be, for there was a great table in the centre, with tall candles making pools of gold on the dark surface of the wood. A crystal dish brimmed with ruddy coated fruit. And a man's hand, resting in one of the circles of candlelight, touched the stem of a crystal goblet, in which the wine lay like liquid amber.

His face was in shadow, but a single gleam from a candle in one sconce behind him touched his hair. At first she thought it was silver, like Uncle Christopher's. Then, as she came nearer she saw that it was gold, paler than her own.

He heard her step at the window and turned quickly. "Who is there?" he asked. His voice was warm, and quiet, like the sound of a slow waterfall in summer. She was not afraid now. She went forward and stood just inside the circle of candlelight but she still could not see his face in the dusk.

"I am Abigail Furnaby," she said.

"Yes," he said, gently, questiongly, and rose. 'Will you sit down?" he asked.

She shook her head.

"My lord, you are young, you are kind. I had thought you would be old. It is my Uncle Christopher who is in peril. And in the morning they will bring him before you, and my father will urge you to cast him into prison. For all that you are so great a sinner, my father will urge you to do this to my Uncle Christopher."

"And is your Uncle Christopher also a sinner?" my lord asked. There was a sound of laughter in his voice but it was still kind.

"Aye, but he is good," Abigail said.

"I see," said my lord. 'There are degrees in sin, then? And what has your uncle done?"

"Oh, many things, my Lord. He has taken wine, and looked upon Jezebels of the street, my mother said, and now he has robbed you."

"Robbed me" exclaimed his lordship, "Of what?"

"He is a poacher, my lord," Abigail said. "But he has given the things to the poor in the countryside," she added defiantly. "They are very, very poor."

"And are they so?" my lord said. He was silent for a moment, then he spoke. "Other good men have done as much before him," he said slowly. "There be just stewards in the world still, little maid."

Then he drew a chair nearer him, by the great candle-lit table.

"Sit here," he commanded. "And I will hear more of this. But first I shall give you," he hesitated, then pushed the slender goblet of wine aside and lifted a dark, bloomy peach from the dish before him.

"I shall give you this," he said, "while you tell me of this good uncle of yours, and why your father would have him so harshly used, for so small an offence!"

He sat so still his face in the shadow, the candlelight touching his hair and the long fine hands folded on the table before him. It was easy to tell him. Here, in this quiet, dim room she knew a rest she had never known. It was as if beauty had folded her wings and was also at rest.

She told him of the sin they found, through all

the length and breadth of the land, people living in riotous pleasure, wine and song and riches, and the wrath of God trembling to fall on them, and they heeding not at all. She told of the towns and villages they had lived in, she and her father and her mother, in that endless, bitter, heart-breaking warefare against evil. They had been a year here, and more. They were not often so long in one place. She told him of Uncle Christopher, man of the sea and of the roads, elbow deep in sin. Uncle Christopher, who sang and told gay tales of the road and kissed every pretty woman he saw, and robbed a rich man's fields to give to the poor.

"He is, then, a greater sinner than I," my lord said. "I have not yet done this last."

"If he were to go away," Abigail said urgently. She leaned forward till the candlelight turned the young, lovely face to downy gold "If he were to promise never to come back here, might he not go. It is high summer. He could not go to prison in high summer, my lord, and the little children run to meet him when he comes."

My lord did not seem to be listening.

"What is your name?" he asked suddenly.

She flushed.

"My name is Abigail," she said again, "but my Uncle Christopher calls me Glorianna."

"Ah, then your hair is red, red and tawny like gold."

She lifted a trembling hand to her cheek, where one soft tendril lay, escaped from her bonnet.

"Yes, it is red, " she said. "And gold," she added in a whisper.

"Then it is certain that your Uncle Christopher is a wise man, and cannot go to prison," he told her.

Abigail rose. "Oh, my lord, you are good!" she cried.

"Another good sinner," he said, and laughed. She liked his laughter; there was no bitterness in it, but something of sorrow.

'Can you not stay with me a little?" he asked. "Am I to have nothing in return."

Abigail closed her eyes. She had expected this.

"I have nothing to give you, my lord, save my thanks, and I will ask the blessing and forgiveness of God for you."

"I have need of both," my lord said, and sighed.

Then he, too, rose.

"Come," he said, and leaned forward and took her hand. For a moment it fluttered like a caged bird, then in his quiet grasp lay still.

He led her from the window to the green terrace again. The darkness was around them now, misty as a flower. She could see the white wraiths of the roses in the garden below; their perfume came in little waves on the dew-cooled air. They stood on the terrace, like children; hand in hand.

"Are you too afraid of God?" he asked her, suddenly.

"We have been redeemed and turned into the

right way," Abigail said, as though it were a well-learned lesson.

"And what of all those who still walk in the thorns outside?" my lord said.

Abigail hesitated. "God is a consuming fire, and will furiously burn up the wicked," she said uncertainly.

"Nay, then He is not," my lord protested. "Hold your breath, little one, and make no sound. For He walks in gardens in the cool of the day. But how few of us know. For there are two things in the world by reason of which we cannot hear Him. And they are great sin and great righteousness."

"It is the little sinners, like your Uncle Christopher, who can hear His feet in the garden," my lord said.

They were quiet, standing there, hand within hand.

Then Abigail said: "My lord, is it so, as my father said, that so great is your wickedness that your eyes blight all on which they look?"

My lord shook his head.

"I do not know," he said. "Yet I wonder that it can be so, for I am blind."

She gave a little cry.

"Not blind, my lord, not that!"

He nodded. "Yes, these ten years now."

"Before I was blind," he said, 'I looked on many things and found them good. But of them all I now mercifully remember only that which was indeed good."

"And what was that, my lord?"

But he shook his head again.

"The ears of the blind hear many things," he said. "Come, and let us listen for the sound of His feet in the garden."